THE GHOSTS OF THE MARIA DORIA

THE GHOSTS OF THE MARIA DORIA

Scott M. Baker

Also by Scott M. Baker

Novels
Operation Majestic
Nurse Alissa vs. the Zombies
Nurse Alissa vs. the Zombies: Escape
Nurse Alissa vs. the Zombies III: Firestorm
Nurse Alissa vs. the Zombies IV: Hunters
Nurse Alissa vs. the Zombies V: Desperate Mission
Nurse Alissa vs. the Zombies VI: Rescue
Nurse Alissa vs. the Zombies VII: On the Road
Burse Alissa vs. the Zombies VIII: New Beginnings
The Chronicles of Paul: A Nurse Alissa Spin-Off
The Ghosts of Eden Hollow
The Ghosts of Salem Village
Frozen World
Shattered World I: Paris
Shattered World II: Russia
Shattered World III: China
Shattered World IV: Japan
Shattered World V: Hell
The Vampire Hunters
Vampyrnomicon
Dominion
Rotter Nation
Rotter Apocalypse
Yeitso

Novellas
Nazi Ghouls From Space
Twilight of the Living Dead

A Schattenseite Book

The Ghosts of the Maria Doria
By Scott M. Baker.
Copyright © 2022. All Rights Reserved.
Print Edition
ISBN-13: 978-1-7365915-6-7

Cover Art © Warren Design

CHAPTER ONE

"I 'M SO DELIGHTED to be here, Captain."

Captain James Fletcher did not know what distracted him more. The oversized brim of the sunhat fluttering in the sea breeze or the unshaved armpits of the female passenger who clasped it tightly to her head.

"We're glad to have you onboard, ma'am."

"My husband and I have been on several of your cruises before, but never on the first sailing of a cruise ship."

"It is a special event. This will be my first time taking out a cruise ship on her maiden voyage."

"Then we both lose our virginities." The woman laughed so loud that everyone on the main deck glanced over to see what all the commotion was about. Her husband rolled his eyes and shook his head, dying from embarrassment. Captain Fletcher did not have that luxury. He forced a smile.

"If you'll excuse me, I'm needed on the bridge."

With a slight bow to the paunchy woman and her humiliated husband, Fletcher departed and made his way along the deck.

Fletcher was excited about taking out the *Maria Doria* on her first cruise. He had been working for Miami Cruise Lines for close to twenty-five years. The company had begun small and purposefully remained so. As the popularity of luxury cruises grew, so did the size of the vessels, becoming ten-deck monstrosities that catered to up to five thousand passengers or more. With the increase in size came a corresponding increase in price. Miami Cruise Lines kept their ships small, limiting them to three hundred passengers and catering to a more moderate-income clientele. They did not provide the glamour or over-the-top amenities of many other lines but of. Still, they offered affordable Caribbean vacations with excellent accommodations, good food, and luxurious ports of call. And half their fleet, like the *Maria Doria*, set sail from New Orleans.

Fletcher enjoyed working for the company. He had fallen in love with the sea when he was a kid and his father took the family every summer to vacation on the coast of Maine. After high school, he did a few tours on lobster and fishing boats, but they did not have the same appeal. A year later, he secured a job with Miami Cruise Lines as a cadet and had been working his way through the ranks since. This job had all the benefits of the tours run by the huge companies—two days at sea, a few overnight ports of call in the Caribbean, and two days back to port—without all the hassles of running a mega-cruise liner manned by a crew of thousands.

Upon arriving on the bridge, Fletcher saw that his four-person crew had gathered along with Michael, their harbor pilot.

"Are we ready for departure?" asked Fletcher.

"We're waiting for you, sir." The answer came from Staff Captain Brendan Sullivan, the ship's second in command, a young officer in his late thirties. Brendan looked like a Hollywood version of a ship captain with blonde hair, deep blue eyes, and exceptionally good looks. His attractiveness made him popular among many of the female passengers who were disappointed to find out that the ocean was Brendan's mistress. The crew respected Brendan because he looked out for them, and the passengers adored him because of his charm. Most important, Brendan was the best second in command Fletcher had served with.

Fletcher stepped over to a middle-aged man sporting a greying beard and offered his hand. "Michael, it's good to see you again."

"Same here." The harbor pilot clasped the extended hand.

"Take her out." With that, Fletcher passed navigational control of the cruise vessel to the pilot.

Michael stood behind the bridge wheel and began the departure. A pair of tugs cautiously pulled the *Maria Doria* away from the dock, turning the ship one hundred and eighty degrees so it faced down the Mississippi River. Once clear of other vessels, the bow tug released its tow line and pulled away, leaving the rear tug still attached in case the cruise ship lost power and needed another vessel to stop it. Michael ordered slow ahead. With a gentle lurch, the *Maria Doria* began its voyage.

Two hours after pushing away from the dock, they had cleared the Mississippi and sailed into the Gulf of Mexico.

Michael stepped away from the control panel. "The ship is yours, Captain."

"Thanks." Fletcher shook the pilot's hand again. "Hopefully, I'll see you in a week when we return."

"I won't be here. I'm flying to Oregon tomorrow. My daughter is getting married this weekend."

"Congratulations. Wish her well for me."

Michael left the bridge, followed by his escort. Several minutes later, he boarded the pilot boat that came alongside and headed back to port.

Fletcher turned to Angelina Rosario, a young woman who had served with him in the past and now made her first cruise as the senior second officer. "Miss Rosario, please take the conn."

"Of course, Captain." Angelina stood in front of the Electronic Chart Display and Information System (ECDIS), the console that incorporates all the main systems and displays the major functions of the ship, such as its speed, compass heading, the pitch of the thrusters, and anything else involving the ship's steering. "Helm, set course bearing 152. Speed twenty-two knots."

"Course set, bearing 152," responded the helmsman, Paolo Aquino, a middle-aged Filipino gentleman who spoke English without an accent. "Speed twenty-two knots."

Fletcher noticed the tension in Angelina's shoulder muscles, which was natural any time an officer took command of such a large vessel for the first time. Even though Fletcher had full confidence in her, he still scanned the surrounding seas for other ships, especially considering the heavy volume of seaborne traffic leaving and entering the mouth of the Mississippi. A cargo vessel approached a few miles ahead to port, its decks stacked with containers. The cargo vessel slowed its speed to take aboard the pilot who would guide it into port. Fletcher waited for Angelina to respond.

A moment later, she called out to the communications officer, "Mister Xu, please contact the approaching vessel via VHF and confirm that we'll be conducting a port to starboard passing."

"Yes, ma'am."

"Helm, maintain heading. Keep a mile distance between us."

"Maintaining heading," responded Paolo.

The two vessels sailed past each other without incident, just as the captain assumed they would. He looked over at Brendan and nodded his approval. His second in command had trained Angelina well.

Twelve minutes later, another vessel approached a few miles ahead to port. Fletcher raised his binoculars to get a better look. It was a large oil tanker, estimated at two hundred and fifty thousand tons.

Angelina issued the command to maintain heading and keep a safe distance and ordered Mister Xu to confirm the port to starboard passing.

When the two ships approached within two miles of each other, the *Maria Doria* suddenly turned fifteen degrees to starboard. Brendan spun around to ascertain the situation, but

Angelina was already on it, moving alongside the helmsman.

"Why aren't we maintaining heading?"

"I don't know." Paolo seemed baffled. "The ship changed course on its own."

"Bring her back to bearing 152."

The helmsman attempted to turn the wheel left and resume course, but it would not budge.

"Why haven't we resumed heading?" asked Angelina.

"The helm is stuck."

Angelina flashed him a derisive glare and stepped over to the wheel, politely ordering the helmsman aside. She took the wheel and tried to correct course, but with no results. After several failed efforts, she turned it to starboard. Again, the ship would not respond and continued moving away from its assigned lane at a fifteen-degree angle.

"I told you," said the helmsman.

Angelina ignored the rebuke and focused on Brendan, who had been observing from the corner of the bridge.

"We have a situation."

Brendan stepped forward. "I have the conn."

His efforts to steer the ship back on course also failed. The rudder remained frozen in place.

"All stop," ordered Brendan.

"All stop." Angelina shut down the engines, allowing the *Maria Doria* to sail on its own momentum.

"Miss Rosario, get on VHF Channel 16 and issue a *securite'* call to all stations informing them we have no rudder control and have shut down our engines."

"Yes, sir."

As Angelina contacted the port authorities, Brendan picked up the phone and dialed the engine room. "Engineering, this is the bridge."

"Why did you cut power to the engines?" asked Ian Sprague, the chief of engineering.

"I had to for safety reasons. We've lost rudder control on

the bridge."

"Hang on." Sprague must have covered the mouthpiece with his hand because his conversations with the department were muffled. After a moment, he came back on. "We have no indications down here that anything is wrong with the rudder."

"Maybe it's a disconnect on the bridge. See if you can bring us back to bearing 152."

"Hang on." Brendan again listened to muffled commands being issued down in engineering before Sprague came back on. "The rudder is not responding down here either. I just dispatched a crew to check on it."

"Keep me posted."

Brendan replaced the receiver in its mount and informed the captain of his exchange with engineering. So much for a successful maiden voyage, thought Fletcher.

"Sir," said Angelina. "New Orleans wants to know if we need assistance returning to port."

Brendan thought for a moment. "Tell them we'll let them know in a few minutes."

Fletcher hated returning early, though safety concerns gave him no other choice. Corporate management would look for someone to take the fall for this economic catastrophe, and all eyes would point at him unless it could be proven that the problem originated from a construction flaw, which would shift blame onto the shipbuilders. Such an ordeal would last months. However, he found it preferable to dealing with a shipload of irate passengers when he had to inform them their cruise had been canceled due to unforeseen circumstances. Somehow, he knew the lady in the floppy hat would not—

"Captain, we have a fire on board." Paolo pointed to the console.

"Where?" asked Brendan.

"The staff mess."

Fletcher switched through the ship's security cameras until the image of the staff mess appeared on the monitor. Only a few personnel occupied the hall, all of them crew members preparing for the next meal, and none of them showing any concern. Everything appeared normal. No flames. Not even smoke. How many other glitches was the ship hiding?

"Should I have the passengers prepare for emergency procedures?" asked Angelina.

Fletcher thought for a second. "We haven't had time to do the muster drill yet. I don't want to cause a panic, especially if it's only a malfunction."

Brendan kept his attention focused on the monitor. "Sir, do you want me to double-check and make certain nothing's wrong?"

"Yes."

Brendan headed for the exit. Just before he left, Fletcher called out to him.

"Something weird is going. Let me know the minute you've checked out the mess."

"Roger that."

Fletcher took over the helm. Thankfully, nothing was in their path, and New Orleans would warn all inbound and outbound vessels to avoid the *Maria Doria*. With luck, nothing else would go wrong. Though the way the day had been going, he half expected to see an iceberg dead ahead.

✕　✕　✕

BRENDAN MADE HIS way to the bow, moving at a brisk pace, but not quickly enough to cause a panic among the crew. The staff mess was located on Deck 4. He reached the door, paused, removed the radio from his belt, and keyed the bridge.

"I'm outside the staff mess."

"The monitor shows nothing's changed inside," answered Angelina.

"Alright. Give me a minute."

As a precaution, Brendan placed the back of his hand

against the door. It felt cool to the touch. He stepped inside.

Nothing appeared out of the ordinary. Seven members of the kitchen staff worked on preparing the evening meal for the crew while two others cleaned tables. Svetlana, a young Russian woman making certain plates and utensils were stacked near the buffet line, glanced up and smiled.

"Can I help you, sir?"

"Is everything okay down here?" Brendan tried to sound as little concerned as possible. "The bridge indicated a fire in the staff mess."

Svetlana turned to the kitchen and yelled something in Russian. A moment later, Oleg, the head chef, stuck his head through the serving window.

"Did you say fire down here?"

Brendan nodded. "The sensors in the bridge indicated there was one."

"You mean like flames?"

"Yes."

Oleg shrugged. "No idea. We not even light stoves yet. Must be wiring. Things today made like Siberian outhouse. Full of shit."

Brendan thought for a moment. Better safe than sorry.

"You're probably right. But can you all step outside for a few minutes while I check?"

"Okay. But make quick, please. We very busy."

When the crew had left, Brendan entered the kitchen. The stoves had not been turned on. There were no open flames. None of the electrical appliances were operating. He even checked the waste baskets and back rooms for anything that might be smoldering but found nothing. As Oleg had so eloquently put it, the alarm system must be malfunctioning. He would love to be a fly on the wall when corporate sat down with the shipbuilder.

Stepping back into the dining area, Brendan looked around for anything unusual, then used the radio to contact the bridge.

"Captain, it's Brendan. There's nothing down here to be alarmed about."

"You're certain about that?" asked Fletcher.

"No need to muster the passengers. The sensors must be as screwed up as the rudder controls. I'm heading back.... Wait a second."

"What's wrong?"

Brendan lowered the radio from his ear and listened. An unusual sound echoed around him. He had been at sea long enough to be familiar with any strange noise a ship could make. This was not one of them. It came from all around, a dull roar, barely audible.

The captain's voice over the radio drowned out the sound. "Brendan, talk to me."

"Just a minute."

Brendan lowered the radio again and listened. The roar grew louder and more distinct. He noticed sweat forming on his forehead, which should not happen in air conditioning. Instinct told him to run. His duty as an executive officer forced him to stay and figure out what was happening. He slowly circled the hall, trying to determine the source of the roar and the heat. Suddenly, both spiked in intensity. Only then did it dawn on him. By now, it was too late. Brendan rushed for the door and stopped. His eyes widened in terror and an anguished scream left his lips.

✕　✕　✕

ON THE BRIDGE, Fletcher watched through the monitor as Brendan stared around the mess hall, a confused expression on his face. He keyed the talk button on the radio.

"Brendan, talk to me."

"Just a minute."

The officer walked around. Suddenly, his expression changed from curiosity to fear. Brendan cried out and fell to the deck. An instant later, the image from the security camera went blank.

"Jesus," muttered Fletcher.

Angelina had also been watching. "Did you see that?"

"Yeah," replied Xu. "Brendan screamed and collapsed."

"No. I was talking just before the camera went out. It... it looked like flames."

✕   ✕   ✕

OLEG AND THE others stood outside the staff mess. He looked at his watch for the fifth time. What was taking Brendan so long? His team still had much to do to prepare for the crew's dinner. If the meals got delayed, then the crew's return to station would be delayed, which meant his ass would be the one chew—

A blood-curdling scream came from inside the mess. Oleg and the others stared at each other, scared and confused. Being closest to the door, Oleg opened it and raced inside, followed by the rest of the staff. They made it only a few feet in before stopping, horrified by the sight that greeted them. Svetlana dropped to her knees and vomited.

Everything in the staff mess was exactly as they had left it a few minutes ago. Everything, that is, except Brendan. Or, more appropriately, what used to be Brendan. The remains of the second in command lay on the deck, burned like a piece of meat that had fallen into a barbecue. The skin had been charred, with the few exposed bones blackened from the flames. Embers still glowed beneath the corpse, and smoke wafted from the limbs. What few facial features remained were frozen in agony.

CHAPTER TWO

"I'M A LITTLE nervous about doing this," Tatyana Reynolds said nervously into her computer's microphone. "I've never done a podcast before."

"You'll do fine." Morgana Thorne did not focus on the camera, instead doing the final preparation work for the show. "Relax. You know this subject better than anyone."

"I'm not used to speaking in front of large groups."

"You're not. You're talking to me. There'll be other people watching." Morgana flashed Tatyana a reassuring smile. "Besides, I don't have a lot of followers. Only a hundred thousand."

Tatyana swallowed hard. If she had known that before-hand, she might not have agreed to come on Morgana's show. Truth be known, she didn't want to do this. She felt as if she was exploiting her gift. But her best friend Julie had insisted. Tatyana had discovered her ability to communicate with the spiritual world while visiting Julie's grandmother's house in Vermont and cleansing it of Kathleen, the evil entity that resided within. After that, her reputation as a ghost hunter... a name she hated... spread throughout New England. During the following year, she agreed to take on several clients to help them with their paranormal situations and make extra money on the side. Being a teacher's assistant while completing your graduate degree did not bring in a lot of income, especially if you enjoyed such luxuries as food, clothing, and shelter.

The cases had been interesting. Several had explanations unrelated to the supernatural, such as skittish people who viewed the creaking of the floor in an old house as the presence of a ghost, noisy plumbing or wind blowing through poorly insulated walls, and, in one case, a raccoon that had taken up residence inside the attic. Most of the cases, however, involved minor hauntings. One was an elderly woman who died in her sleep one night, and her spirit still thought she lived there. Another had concerned a suicide victim who hanged himself in the basement; his spirit remained bound to the house and his tormented soul passed on his anguish to the current occupants. These were easy to send on to the afterlife. Only one couple did not ask that the house be cleansed. Two gentlemen with an eight-year-old adopted son had been haunted since moving into their new home by an entity that kept on annoying them. It turned out that the spirit belonged to that of a seven-year-old girl who had died of cancer and only wanted to get the new family to spend time with her; they allowed it to remain, and she and the son played together.

Despite trying to keep a low profile, notoriety came to Tatyana after the incident several months ago in Salem, Massachusetts. She had discovered and exorcised the spirit of a nineteenth, unknown victim of the infamous witch trials, a woman who had been executed in a sadistic manner. Because of the nature of the case, city officials could not keep the incident covered up. Within a month, the story was featured on every local news station, reported in dozens of newspapers, and even made it to a few network cable news shows. After that, Tatyana had more potential clients than she could handle. On the plus side, she could now afford to buy her own car and rent a decent apartment with a yard for Nostradamus. On the downside, her paranormal activities severely cut into the time she should be using to complete her dissertation.

That's when Julie came up with the idea of going live on Morgana's podcast, reasoning that the more people who knew about Tatyana, the better her chances of getting more lucrative clients who could pay better. The idea appealed to Tatyana.

More money for fewer jobs would allow her to manage her time better. She didn't want to throw away all the years she worked on getting her degree. And the money would help pay off the student loans she had accrued. She would miss coming to the assistance of those who needed her, those dealing with legitimate paranormal situations but who didn't have the financial means to cope with the issue. Once she graduated, she could always go back to help them.

"We're all set." Morgana switched her concentration fully on Tatyana. "We'll go live in a minute. I'll run the introduction to the show and then introduce you. I'll give you a few minutes to talk about yourself before I start the interview. Any questions?"

"Nope."

Morgana smiled. A moment later, the red LIVE button appeared on Tatyana's computer screen. She focused on her video feed for the first time and almost gasped. She had spent an hour putting on make-up and picking out the appropriate attire but never thought to check the lighting by her desk. Julie had suggested using one of those LED ring lights, but the illumination from it gave an eerie glow to her face, making Tatyana appear like an apparition. Tatyana quickly switched on the desk lamp, which made it worse, whiting out her features. Frustrated, she turned off the light.

The lights in the ceiling fan came on, startling her. Tatyana glanced over to see Nick, her ghostly colleague, moving away from the wall switch. As always, he wore his pristine World War II-era navy uniform, the same one he had on when murdered. She always mused about what Nick would look like if he had died in a hospital wearing one of those open-ended gowns.

"What are you doing here?"

"Providing moral support. I can sense you're nervous." Nick sat on the sofa directly behind her. Nostradamus, Tatyana's Pitbull, jumped on the couch clutching his favorite chew toy, a rubber ghost that squeaked. The dog curled up beside Nick.

"You're welcome to stay, just don't bother me. I'm nervous enough as it is."

"Have I ever bothered you?"

Tatyana rolled her eyes and turned her attention back to the screen. Damn, the overhead lighting did the trick. She looked good.

The countdown to the end of the taped introduction reached five seconds when Tatyana's cellphone pinged. She leaned over and glanced at it. It was a text from Julie.

Good luck, girl. You'll rock this.

"Good evening, ladies and gentlemen. I'm your host of Wyrd Paranormal, Morgana Thorne. Tonight, we have a special guest, Tatyana Reynolds, the paranormal investigator involved in the recent incident involving the unknown victim of the Salem Witch Trials. Before we begin, subscribe to this podcast and hit like at the end if you enjoyed the content. Now, Tatyana, tell us a little something about yourself."

"Well," Tatyana cleared her throat and breathed deeply. This was scarier than dealing with evil entities. "As you know, I'm a part-time paranormal investigator. Full time, I'm attending Dartmouth College finishing off my Ph.D."

"What subject?"

"European History."

"Before becoming a paranormal investigator, did you study the history of witchcraft or the paranormal?"

"No. I never had any interest in either until about a year ago when I visited a mansion in northern Vermont with several entities trapped inside. They reached out to me."

"That's Julie's grandmother, correct?"

"Yes."

"Why did they reach out to you?"

Tatyana smiled. "One of the entities, Nick—"

"She mentioned me," he said to Nostradamus. The dog barked.

"—realized I could communicate with the spirit world and asked for my help in ridding the house of a malevolent ghost that kept them trapped there."

"And you were successful?"

"Yes."

Morgana chuckled. "You seem surprised."

"It was a life-changing moment. One day, I'm teaching history to college students who don't care about the subject, and the next, I'm exorcising an evil entity from an old woman's house."

"And after that, you continued to do paranormal investigations and cleansings."

"Yes."

"Would you say it's your calling?"

Tatyana thought for a moment. "I don't know if I'd refer to it as a calling. I enjoy helping people who have, or believe they have, ghosts in their home or business."

"Let's talk about what our listeners are most interested in. That's your involvement with the exorcism of the ghost from Salem. How did you...."

Tatyana quickly fell into her groove and enjoyed herself. She talked about her encounter with Eliza Adams, the unknown victim of the Salem witchcraft hysteria, going into explicit detail about what transpired. That took up nearly the entire hour. Morgana then began asking questions posted in the comments section by the viewers, and there were quite a few. Half a dozen people accused her of being a fraud who used supernatural "mumbo jumbo," as one person put it, to dupe the gullible. Most of those watching were supportive. One gentleman from Ohio asked if she could fly out to help him with a haunted bar he owned; Tatyana politely declined. A woman from Utah wanted to know when Tatyana would get her own reality TV show. One boy from Arkansas pointed out Nostradamus sitting in the background and wondered why the dog kept staring at the empty seat beside him. A teenage girl from Arizona felt she had the ability to talk with ghosts and wanted to know how to perfect them; Tatyana told the teenager to pass Morgana her email so she could reach out privately.

The show had gone forty-five minutes over its usual hour when Morgana wrapped up. She thanked Tatyana for being on, thanked her viewers for tuning in, and reminded them to like and subscribe before ending the podcast. Both women waited until the red LIVE button switched to BROADCAST ENDED.

"That was a great show," exclaimed Morgana. "One of the highest viewership yet."

"I'm glad. I enjoyed myself."

"I told you you'd do well."

"So did I," Nick chimed in from the sofa.

"I'll have to have you back sometime," said Morgana.

"I'd like that."

"Before you go, do you want that young woman's email?"

"Of course. I don't mind chatting with her."

Morgana passed it along to Tatyana, who scribbled it down on a piece of paper.

"One more thing," said Morgana, a bit hesitant. "During the podcast, I received an email from someone named Giselle begging me to pass you her phone number. She desperately wants to talk to you. Claims she has an urgent paranormal situation that she wants to discuss."

"Sounds like a nutjob."

Morgana scrunched her lips. "I don't think so. I've dealt with more than my fair share of the tinfoil hat crowd in this job. Giselle's email seemed serious and desperate. She gave me her cellphone number and asked me to give it to you. But it's your call."

Nick shook his head. "Don't do it."

Without thinking, she responded, "Why?"

"Why what?" asked Morgana, confused.

"Sorry. I was thinking to myself."

"I have a bad feeling about this," added Nick.

"Give me the number," said Tatyana. "That takes you off the hook in case she gets in touch with you again."

"I appreciate that." Morgana read the phone number, and Tatyana wrote it down underneath the teenager's email address. They said their goodbyes and closed the streaming service.

Tatyana spun her chair around to face Nick. "What were you saying?"

"I have a bad feeling about this. I don't know why. My gut tells me not to call."

"Aren't you the least bit curious?"

"I've lived in this realm world for close to eighty years. There's not much I'm curious about anymore." Nick stood. "Do what you want. You will anyways. Just be careful before you accept any job offers."

"Will I see you tomorrow?"

"Of course. Bothering you is the highlight of my day." Nick smiled at Tatyana and then turned to Nostradamus. "See you later, boy."

Nostradamus barked twice as Nick morphed into a cloud of mist that slowly dissipated.

Tatyana swung her chair back to the desk and picked up the paper. It was late, almost eleven o'clock. She'd email the teenage girl before going to class in the morning. Yet the phone number called to her. It had a 786-area code. Tatyana called up Google and typed it into the search bar. The area code belonged to Miami. Now she was more intrigued than ever. She glanced over at Nostradamus.

"Wag your tail if you think I should call the number."

The Pitbull wagged his tail. Tatyana knew it was a rigged

election. He wagged his tail at everything. Curiosity got the better of her, and she dialed the number on her cellphone.

A nearly frantic female voice answered on the second ring. "Is this Tatyana Reynolds?"

The greeting caught Tatyana by surprise. "How did you know?"

"I didn't. I was hoping it'd be you. I'm Giselle DeMarco, public relations director for Miami Cruise Lines. I need to talk to you as soon as possible."

CHAPTER THREE

WHEN GISELLE SAID as soon as possible, she did not mean a phone call or a video conference that night. She requested a one-on-one with Tatyana and asked if they could meet within a few days, hopefully, the following afternoon. Giselle would only say she wanted to discuss a delicate issue that could only be handled with Tatyana's expertise, stressing she could not provide details over an open line. Giselle even offered to send a private plane to bring her to Miami. Because Tatyana had no idea who this woman was and what she wanted, she politely deferred. Giselle then asked... almost pleaded... to meet Tatyana somewhere near Dartmouth College. The woman's insistence sparked a flame of curiosity in Tatyana, so she relented and said she'd meet Giselle after class at four o'clock at the Starbucks on South Main Street.

Now Tatyana sat at an isolated two-seat table near the front door to Starbucks, waiting for Giselle. And wondering why she had agreed to this. For a woman about to earn her Ph.D., arranging a meeting with someone she knew nothing about seemed stupid. Giselle... if that was her real name... was likely some wacko who saw her on the podcast last night and wanted to relate her stories about ghosts, Bigfoot, and aliens. At least Tatyana chose a public venue in case this meeting went....

A middle-aged woman opened the door and stepped inside. She wore a red dress and black heels and appeared profession-al. Tatyana suddenly realized she had no idea what Giselle looked like. The woman paused and glanced around. Tatyana started to raise her hand when the woman's eyes widened. A smile pierced her lips. She made her way to the table behind Tatyana, where a middle-aged man in a business suit stood and hugged the woman. The two sat down and chatted excitedly.

Tatyana checked her watch. It read 4:22. You only waited fifteen minutes for a professor and twenty minutes for a professor with a Ph.D. This was ridiculous. She should have realized that when Giselle promised to send a private jet and fly her to Miami. Tatyana chastised herself for falling for this bullshit. Well, at least she made a fool of herself here where she could get a cup of coffee and quietly skulk away rather than at the airport where she would—

"Excuse me, are you Tatyana Reynolds?"

Tatyana glanced over her shoulder. A woman in her early thirties stood beside the table. She was tall, approximately five feet eleven inches, with a shapely physique that reminded Tatyana of a centerfold model. The woman filled out her blue sweater nicely and, if the woman had not been wearing jeans and boots, Tatyana guessed her legs would be just as attractive. Wavy blonde hair flowed over her shoulders, framing a face as beautiful as her body. When the woman smiled, she must look stunning. Only now her blue eyes and jaw were etched with consternation.

"I'm Tatyana." She stood and clasped the woman's hand.

"I thought so. I recognized you from last night's podcast. I'm Giselle DeMarco." The woman reached into her back pocket, pulled out a leather ID holder, and flipped it open. Inside sat an identity card from Miami Cruise Lines with her photo. "Just so you know I'm legitimate."

"Thanks." Tatyana smiled and motioned to the seat across from her.

Giselle sat down. "I'm sure you had your concerns."

"To be honest, I did."

"I don't blame you. I came on a little strong last night. After watching you on the podcast and researching your involvement in the Salem incident, I knew you were the right person for the job."

"What job is that?" Curiosity started to get the better of Tatyana.

"Before we get to that…." Giselle placed the briefcase bag she carried on the table and opened it. She rummaged through the papers for a few seconds before pulling out a single sheet and a pen which she placed in front of Tatyana. "I need you to sign this."

Tatyana pulled the sheet toward her and read it. "A non-disclosure agreement?"

"I know it seems bizarre, but corporate insisted you sign that before we talk. What I'm about to tell you is extremely proprietary and cannot be discussed. By signing it, you're under no obligation to Miami Cruise Lines. You only have to promise to keep this conversation between us."

Tatyana read through the NDA and didn't see anything out of the ordinary, so she signed and dated the document, then slid it back to Giselle.

"Thank you." The woman took the piece of paper and returned it to the briefcase bag, an expression of relief on her face.

"I'm curious why a cruise line needs a paranormal investigator. Are we talking a haunted cruise ship?"

Giselle used her right hand to rub her forehead. "Honestly, I don't know."

"Then why come to me?"

"Three weeks ago, we had an incident aboard one of our cruise liners, the *Maria Doria*, our newest vessel on its maiden voyage out of New Orleans. Everything was going well until the liner entered the shipping lanes. The captain lost navigational control."

"Sounds more like an engineering issue."

"A few minutes after the liner lost navigation, the control panel reported a fire in the staff mess. None of the security cameras indicated anything was wrong, so the staff captain went down to check on it personally. He reported nothing unusual in the area but ushered the kitchen staff into the main corridor while he checked. According to the kitchen staff and those monitoring his activities on the bridge, the staff captain was on his way out of the dining area when he bent over in pain and screamed." Giselle removed a set of five 8x10 color photographs from her briefcase bag. "When the kitchen staff rushed back in to check, this is what they found."

Tatyana took the photos and examined them. They each showed a charred body from different angles. The limbs were curled up in a near fetal position as if the victim had tried to protect himself.

"What caused this? A flash fire?"

"No. Look at the furniture around the body. It's untouched. The only part of the staff mess scorched were the tiles directly beneath the body."

Tatyana studied the photographs, concentrating on the area around the corpse. As Giselle had mentioned, there were no indications of a fire nearby. Not even the linen napkins were singed. She displayed an expression of confusion.

"You'd think that if a body burned for that length of time, the fire would spread."

"That's one of the bizarre things about this case. It was less than five seconds from when the staff captain screamed until they found the body like this." Giselle fished a report in a leather binder out of the bag and handed it to Tatyana. "The crew testimony is all in here. Everyone's stories matched."

Tatyana thumbed through the report for several minutes. "What could cause a fire so intense it burned a body this bad so quickly?"

"We have no answer to that. Once the liner returned to port, dozens of investigators swarmed the ship from every agency imaginable. The New Orleans Fire Department. The Department of Transportation. The shipbuilders. Corporate even hired three sets of engineers from different companies to conduct independent investigations. None of them could find a cause for what happened. A few theories postulated that maybe one of the stoves erupted and set the staff captain on fire, but the bridge crew swore they saw him in the mess area alive and well a second before the camera went out."

"What did the autopsy reveal?"

"Nothing. There were no alcohol or drugs in his system, and the coroner detected nothing flammable on his remains or the tiles around him. One of the corporate lawyers even suggested spontaneous combustion."

Tatyana glanced up from the report and fixed her gaze on Giselle. "Really?"

"Corporate is desperate to find a plausible answer that takes the burden of responsibility off us." Giselle paused. "What's really strange is that right after the staff captain died, full navigational control returned to the liner."

"And you think there's something paranormal going on, which is why you came to me."

"I don't know what to think." Giselle sighed. "Every other possibility has been examined and dismissed, from technical malfunctions to foul play to suicide. One of the bigwigs in Miami suggested the possibility of a ghost, and the CEO ordered me to find an investigator who could assess the situation. That's why I was watching the podcast last night. I'm looking for someone credible, someone who is well respected and won't turn this into a publicity stunt. The last thing the shareholders want is to see this show up on *Ghost Busters*. I did a lot of research, especially on you. The way you handled the ghost in Salem makes me think you're perfect for this job."

"I don't know." Though the idea sounded intriguing, Tatyana felt certain this would be a wild goose chase. She still had classes to teach. "Where is the *Maria Doria* now?"

"Docked in New Orleans."

"That's too far for me to—"

"Corporate is willing to pay you $50,000 to do a paranormal reading on the liner."

Well, maybe chasing geese could pay off after all. "Are you serious?

Giselle nodded. "I am. Plus expenses."

"That's a lot of money."

"Not to the corporation. They're desperate to get this resolved."

"They want to find the answer?"

"They want *an* answer." Giselle leaned a little closer. "Corporate is looking only at the bottom line. The cruise industry is still recovering from the pandemic, and the smaller cruise lines are suffering the most. *Maria Doria* is our newest liner and had the most bookings. We lost a fortune having to cancel the cruise and refund the money. Unless they reach a viable conclusion about what caused the staff captain's death, they can't put the liner back into service, which means the season's a wash. Plus, local media is breathing down corporate's neck demanding answers. Every other option has been explored, and the review board still can't find a way to resolve the issue. It'll mean bankruptcy if Miami Cruise Lines has to pull the ship out of service."

"Does the board really believe the incident was supernatural in origin?"

"To be upfront with you, most think the idea of a haunted cruise liner is bullshit. Those pushing this option are in a panic. The consensus is that if we exhaust all options, no matter how unlikely they may be, it'll be good for the company's reputation. All they want is for you to come out and take a tour of the ship."

A shiver went down Tatyana's spine. "I don't know. I'm scared of water."

"Really?"

"I never learned how to swim. The thought of being aboard a cruise ship terrifies me."

"It'll stay in port if that's any incentive."

Tatyana contemplated the proposal.

Giselle repressed a sigh, not of frustration but defeat. "I know this whole thing sounds bizarre. It does to me, too. But you said on the podcast last night that you've done paranormal readings of locations presumed to be haunted that turned out not to be the case. This is going to be the same deal. You'll spend an afternoon aboard the ship, tell the board there's no paranormal activity, and you're home the next day. Corporate is happy, your reputation remains intact, and you make $50,000 plus a free trip to New Orleans."

Tatyana ran the entire scenario through her head, trying to find the flaws, but she could not. She taught classes only on Tuesday and Thursday, and tomorrow was Friday, so that gave her four days to fly down, conduct her investigation, hopefully cajole a night in New Orleans, and still be back in time to teach her next class. And she certainly could use the money.

"I'll do it."

Giselle's face lit up. "Thank you."

"My pleasure." Tatyana paused. "Can I bring Nostradamus with me?"

The woman's eyes narrowed. "Who's Nostradamus?"

"My Pitbull. Animals are attuned to spirits. He's like an early warning system."

"Is he friendly around other people?"

"Very."

"Then it's fine with me. I'm sure the captain won't mind."

"Thanks. What next?"

Giselle closed her briefcase bag. "I'm staying down the street at the Hanover Inn. Give me your address and I'll pick you up at eight tomorrow morning. My plane is at the Lebanon Municipal Airport. The pilot will fly us back. Pack enough things for three days. You'll be back Sunday night. It's a free weekend in New Orleans."

"That sounds nice."

"You should be there during Madi Gras." Giselle winked

and stood. "I'll see you in the morning. Oh, and bring your bank account information with you so I can deposit your fee."

Tatyana watched Giselle leave via the front door and turn right toward the hotel. She waited a few minutes, finishing her iced tea and admiring her good fortune. She hadn't been on vacation in a while and had never been to New Orleans. Hell, she had never flown on a private jet before. This promised to be a fun weekend.

CHAPTER FOUR

TATYANA HAD HER suitcase and carry-on on the bed as she packed. Nostradamus curled up on the pillows, a wary eye on her. Every time she placed an article of clothing in the suitcase or slid something into her travel bag, the dog's eyes went from what was packed to his mistress. Somehow, he knew she would be going on a trip.

She circled around the side of the bed, leaned over, and petted the dog. "Don't worry, boy. I'm taking you with me."

Nostradamus barked once and wagged his tail. Tatyana scratched behind his ears. He raised his head and licked her face.

"Get a room," said a familiar voice behind her.

Tatyana turned around. Nick sat in her reading chair in the corner, his legs crossed and resting on a hassock.

"This *is* my room." She grinned and went back to packing. "What are you doing here?"

"Checking to see if you were really going to New Orleans."

"Sure. Why not?"

"I don't like the idea."

"What's not to like? I get an all-expense paid trip down south plus a big chunk of money to walk around a cruise ship and tell them there are no ghosts aboard. It's a sweet deal."

"I'm not saying it isn't." Nick shrugged. "I just have a gut feeling this is more complicated than it seems."

"I thought you didn't have physical feelings."

"Then call it intuition or a sixth sense, whatever you want. There's something not right about this. I sensed it on Giselle."

27

Tatyana paused and raised an eyebrow. "You were spying on me?"

"Only when it comes to your paranormal activities. Remember, I was here when you got the phone call from her. Did you think I wouldn't eavesdrop?"

"I'm surprised you didn't make your presence known at Starbucks. You like to distract me when I'm busy." She resumed packing. "So, what were you saying about Giselle? You don't trust her?"

"It's not Giselle. She's stressed out and a bundle of emotions. I picked up an aura that attached itself to her. I don't know. Something…." Nick couldn't find the right words.

"Evil?"

"Angry. Malicious. Vindictive. I don't know how to describe it. It was faint. She had only been tainted with it, probably by being on the cruise ship. It gave me an unsettling feeling."

"Like your ex-wife?"

"It's hard to tell without being closer to the source, but I think it's more malevolent than Kathleen."

The memories of that night cleansing Kathleen from the mansion in Eden Hollow brought back bitter memories. That had been Tatyana's first experience with the paranormal and almost her last. She hoped Nick was wrong about there being a presence aboard the *Maria Doria* even more malevolent than Kathleen.

"I guess we'll find out tomorrow night." Tatyana finished with her travel bag and placed it on the floor at the foot of the bed. "Will you be able to follow me to New Orleans? It's pretty far from here."

"I'm spiritually connected to you, so I can home in on wherever you are any time I want."

"You're good at that." Tatyana stepped over to the dresser, pulled open the top drawer, removed two pairs of black lace panties with matching bras, and tossed them into the suitcase.

Nick grinned. "Awfully fancy for a business trip."

"That's it. Time to go."

Nick pretended to be hurt. "I only want to keep you company."

"That's what Nostradamus is for." Tatyana moved toward Nick and shooed him away as if he was an obnoxious pest. "Go. I need to get some rest. I have a long day tomorrow."

"Fine. I'll see you in New Orleans." Nick stood and straightened out his uniform. "Don't forget to bring a lace nightgown."

Tatyana grabbed a throw pillow from the bed and lovingly threw it at him, but Nick had already turned into a mist and disappeared. Nostradamus raised his head and tilted it to one side, always confused at Nick's departures. Tatyana picked up the pillow, placed it on the bed, and held the dog's face in her hands.

"Don't worry, boy. He'll be back."

That was something Tatyana could count on.

She only hoped his premonition about what they would find aboard the *Maria Doria* was wrong.

CHAPTER FIVE

A LIMOUSINE PICKED up Tatyana in front of her apartment at eight o'clock sharp. The chauffeur stepped out of the driver's seat and opened the rear door.

"Good morning, ma'am."

"How are you today?"

"Fine, thank you. Can I take your bags?"

"That'd be great."

"Miss DeMarco is at the airport overseeing the preparations for the flight. Please, have a seat."

Twenty minutes later, the limo parked beside a Gulfstream G280. The chauffeur got out and opened the rear door. "Miss DeMarco is already on board. You can join her. I'll take care of your luggage."

Tatyana made her way to the boarding stairs. Nostradamus ran ahead and bounded up ahead of her. A flight attendant met him at the entrance of the plane. She broke into a broad smile and crouched.

"Aren't you a handsome boy."

Nostradamus barked in agreement.

The flight attendant stood and extended her hand. "You must be Tatyana."

"I am." Tatyana clasped her hand.

"I'm Veronica. Welcome on board. Miss DeMarco is in the cabin waiting. We'll be taking off as soon as your luggage is stored. Can I get you anything to drink? I'm making a mimosa for Miss DeMarco."

"That'd be nice. Thanks."

Nostradamus ran in ahead of Tatyana. He sniffed around the cabin before rushing over to greet Giselle. To the woman's credit, she leaned forward and scratched the dog behind his ears. The Pitbull's tail wagged furiously. Tatyana followed and sat down in the seat opposite Giselle. The woman stopped petting Nostradamus, who ran over and jumped onto one of the bench seats along the side of the plane.

"Morning," said Giselle. "Did you get a good sleep?"

"I did."

"You'll need it."

"This is a lot better than coach." Tatyana wiggled her behind into the plush seat and spread out her arms. "I could get used to this."

"It gets old after a while." Giselle removed an iPad from her briefcase bag. "Do you have your bank account info?"

"Yeah." Tatyana reached into her rear pants pocket and withdrew a folded piece of paper that she handed to Giselle. The woman called up the Internet and entered the information. After a few minutes, she shut down the iPad and handed back the piece of paper. "The money has been deposited in your account."

Tatyana reached for her cell phone but stopped.

"Go ahead," said Giselle. "You can check. It's okay."

Removing the cell phone, Tatyana checked her bank account. Sure enough, the money had been deposited from Miami Cruise Lines. She stared at the amount for a moment, amazed at the figure.

"Why don't you ask Giselle if she's been aboard the cruise ship."

Tatyana glanced over to the bench where Nostradamus lay curled up. Nick sat beside the dog, his legs crossed, his left arm on the seat back.

"Go ahead. Ask her."

Tatyana shushed him.

Giselle looked confused. "I didn't say anything."

31

"I was telling Nostradamus to be quiet."

Giselle turned to the dog. "He's asleep."

Tatyana shrugged.

Nick widened his eyes and nodded toward Giselle, mouthing the words, "Ask her."

"Giselle, have you been aboard the *Maria Doria*? Since the accident?"

"For a few hours. I accompanied the fire investigation team."

Nick smirked. Tatyana ignored him.

"Did you experience anything?"

"Are you asking if I saw any ghosts?"

"Not necessarily. Did you walk into any exceptionally cold areas, or did you feel any sense of foreboding or uneasiness?"

"No. Sorry."

"No problem. Just asking."

Veronica came out of the kitchen area holding a tray with two mimosas and placed them on the table in front of each woman. "We'll be taking off in a few minutes. Please fasten your seatbelts until we're at cruising altitude. Do you need anything before we depart?"

"We're all set," said Giselle. As Veronica returned to the kitchen area, Giselle turned to Tatyana. "Sit back and relax. We should be in New Orleans in five hours."

✕   ✕   ✕

THE GULFSTREAM LANDED at Louis Armstrong International Airport early in the afternoon. The moment Tatyana stepped off the plane, the heat and humidity engulfed her like an evil entity. She rarely experienced weather this oppressive in northern New Hampshire. Another limousine waited on the tarmac. Tatyana sighed with relief when she entered the air-conditioned cabin. The limousine took them to the Port of New Orleans along the Mississippi River, passed through the

32

security gate, and slowly made its way along the pier, passing three large cruise liners.

Tatyana looked out the window at the ships towering ten stories above her. She shivered.

"Is anything wrong?" asked Giselle.

"Ships like this creep me out. How do they not capsize?"

"I get asked that a lot," the woman chuckled. "It's because the top is mostly open space. All the heavy parts of the ship—the engines, fuel tanks, ballast, water and waste storage, and supplies—are below the waterline. The center of gravity on these ships is low. You'd have to tip one over at more than a forty-five-degree angle to capsize it. To do that, one of these liners would have to be caught in a severe storm with no way to control the ship. Don't worry. We're not going to be heading out to sea."

"That's true." Tatyana tried not to sound too relieved. "Which one is the *Maria Doria*?"

"That one down there."

Giselle pointed to the last vessel. A smaller liner was moored to the dock. It measured five hundred feet in length and had only four passenger levels above the main deck and two below. It appeared half the size of the other liners.

"These other ships are for the more expensive cruises," explained Giselle. "The larger ships belong to other cruise lines. At full capacity, the *Maria Doria* carries three hundred passengers and a crew of two hundred."

"How does that compare to the other ships?"

"Most carry three thousand passengers and a crew of seven hundred. Some of the largest liners can carry over six thousand passengers and two thousand crew members."

The limo stopped in front of the gangplank leading to the *Maria Doria*. The chauffeur jumped out and opened the door. Giselle climbed out first, followed by Tatyana and Nostradamus. A crew member rushed from the ship to the back of the limo to gather the luggage.

"Won't I be staying at a hotel?" asked Tatyana.

"We're setting you up in one of the Deluxe Suites on board. I figured it would be easier and save a lot of travel time. I know you're afraid of the water. If you want, I can get you a hotel in town."

"On board will be fine."

"Follow me, please." Giselle then turned to the driver. "Do you mind waiting?"

"Not a problem, ma'am."

Giselle led the way up the gangway. A young, attractive woman wearing a white uniform waited for them at the hatch. She was in her late twenties, with tanned skin and long, brunette hair pinned in a bun. As the two women approached, she stepped forward and offered her hand.

"Miss DeMarco, Miss Reynolds. Welcome aboard. I'm Angelina Rosario, the senior second officer."

Handshakes and pleasantries were exchanged, including the obligatory petting of Nostradamus. Angelina stepped toward the main corridor and motioned for the ladies to follow. "Captain Fletcher is waiting for you on the bridge. If you'll follow me, please."

Nostradamus paused every few feet to sniff all the new smells, then ran ahead to catch up with his mistress.

Angelina glanced over her shoulder at Tatyana. "Miss DeMarco mentioned you're a paranormal investigator. Is that true?"

"It is."

"Do you think the ship is haunted?"

Giselle jumped in. "We'll have to see where the investigation leads."

"Of course."

"Where did the accident take place?" asked Tatyana.

"Two levels below us in the staff mess. I'll take you there after we meet the captain."

"Have you had any similar incidents since that first one?"

Angelina took her head. "No. But then again, we've been in dock since that night. And there's only a skeleton crew on board."

"And no one was able to come up with a cause for that flash fire?"

"Nothing that I'm aware of. I'm assuming it was one of those freak accidents you sometimes hear about." Angelina stopped at an elevator and ushered the others inside.

Five minutes later, they entered the bridge. A man Tatyana assumed to be the captain stood by the ECDIS console reading from a clipboard a junior officer had handed him. He was tall and thin, a little over six feet and weighing no more than one hundred and fifty pounds. She guessed his age to be in the early to mid-fifties based on the tinges of grey in his red hair and short, well-groomed beard. He exuded seriousness and professionalism. As they entered, he lifted his head and nodded, then went back to reading. Once finished, he handed the clipboard back to the junior officer and crossed the bridge.

"Miss DeMarco, good to see you again." He offered his hand to Tatyana. "I'm Captain Fletcher. You must be Miss Reynolds."

"I am." She shook his hand. "It's a pleasure to meet you."

Nostradamus barked.

Fletcher held out his hand to the Pitbull, who placed his paw in it. The captain smiled. "And who is your companion?"

"That's Nostradamus. I hope you don't mind me bringing him on board. Like me, he's attuned to any spiritual presence and helps with my investigations."

"It's not a problem at all. If you want, Angelina will escort you to the staff mess so you can start your investigation."

"If it's okay with you, captain, I'd like to do that later to-night. Preferably around three in the morning?"

"Why so late?"

"The spirit world is most active at that time. If you have any presence aboard your ship, my best chance of detecting it is at three in the morning."

"And if you don't detect any," began Fletcher, "then the chances are good there are no ghosts?"

"Exactly."

"That's fine with me. Miss DeMarco?"

Giselle suppressed a frown. "I can come back."

"We'll meet here on the bridge at two-thirty," decided Fletcher. "Angelina, will you show Miss Reynolds and her companion to their suite?"

"Of course, sir." Then, to Tatyana, "Follow me, please."

$$\times \quad \times \quad \times$$

TATYANA'S SUITE WAS located on Deck Three overlooking the Mississippi. It consisted of a large sitting room with a sofa overlooking the river, a spacious bedroom with a king-size bed and a balcony, and a dressing room. Upon seeing the couch, Nostradamus raced across the room and jumped up, curling into a ball on the cushions.

"I'm so sorry," Tatyana said, embarrassed. "Get down from there. You'll get fur on it."

"He's fine." Angelina smiled. "You don't want to know what type of stuff gets all over the furniture. We have an excellent cleaning crew."

"Thank you."

"Kevin already placed your luggage in the bedroom. Our kitchen isn't open, but dial room service if you want something to eat. I'll have someone on duty. They can order out for you. They'll also take your dog for a walk if you want."

"You're too kind."

"Believe me, it's our pleasure. You're doing the cruise line a huge favor." Angelina made her way to the door and paused. "I'll be back to get you a quarter after two."

As the door closed, Nick's voice sounded behind Tatyana. "Man, this is much nicer than the last time I was at sea. This suite is bigger than the captain's quarters aboard a battleship."

"I'm glad you approve." Tatyana joined him by the window. "Have you been here long?"

"Just arrived. Do you sense any paranormal activity?"

"Nothing. Not even a background hum. I think this investigation is going to be quick and simple." Tatyana thought a moment. "Do you still have that feeling of impending disaster?"

Nick nodded. "Yeah. But I can't figure out why."

"Let's hope you're wrong. Now, if you'll excuse me, I want to grab a nap since I'm going to be up all night. I assume you'll join me later?"

"Of course. I'm going to tour the ship and see if I can sense anything. See you in a few hours."

Nick disappeared into a cloud of mist, causing Nostradamus to tilt his head again in confusion.

"Come on, boy. This heat and humidity sucked the energy out of me. Let's lie down for a while. We have a busy night ahead of us."

CHAPTER SIX

TATYANA STOOD ON the balcony of her suite looking out over the Mississippi River, studying McDonough and Algiers Point across the river. Even at this late hour, lights still shone in numerous houses. Off to her right, the Crescent City Connection Bridge spanned the river. Because it had been built too low for larger cruise liners and cargo ships to sail under, these vessels docked north of the structure in what became the bustling port area. Vehicles still drove across the bridge in large numbers. Tatyana marveled how New Orleans never seemed to rest. It bustled twenty-four hours a day, a sharp contrast to her sleepy little college town in northern New Hampshire. She wondered how much paranormal energy flowed through this city.

Certainly, a lot more than aboard the *Maria Doria*.

A knock sounded on the cabin door. Tatyana checked her watch. Exactly 2:15. The crew was efficient.

Tatyana exited the bedroom, calling for Nostradamus to follow. When she opened the door, Angelina waited.

"Good evening, Miss Reynolds. I hope you had a good rest."

"I did. And please, call me Tatyana."

"Of course." The officer smiled. "The captain requested you meet with him before we escort you to the staff mess."

"Lead the way."

A few minutes later, they entered the bridge. Captain Fletcher was there along with Gisella and three other officers who stood by the ECDIS console. The captain greeted

Tatyana.

"I hope your accommodations are acceptable."

"They're excellent. Thank you."

"Before we begin, I wanted to go over a few procedures with you." Fletcher motioned to one of the officers. "This is Safety Officer Jose Hernandez. He's going to be monitoring the fire detection equipment. The last time we were at sea, the detectors malfunctioned and recorded a fire in the staff mess. Mister Sullivan went down to investigate, which was when the accident occurred. If we see any indications of a fire, we'll warn you immediately so you can evacuate the area. And please, no heroics. If a malfunction caused this, I don't want anyone else getting hurt. Understood?"

Tatyana nodded.

"Miss Rosario and Miss DeMarco will accompany you to the staff mess. Before we begin, do you have any questions?"

"Just one. Other than Mister Sullivan, did anyone ever die aboard this ship? A crew member or a passenger?"

"No. I would have immediately been notified. Besides, the crew had only been aboard a few weeks, and the passengers had embarked that afternoon."

"What about during construction?"

"Not that I'm aware of." The captain looked over to Giselle. "Do you know anything about that?"

"No," Giselle responded. "I can ask corporate about it in the morning."

Fletcher nodded and switched his attention to Tatyana. "Is there anything else?"

"I have no more questions." Tatyana looked at her watch. "Let's get this started. It's almost three."

Fletcher nodded. "Good luck, ladies. I'll be here on the bridge if you need me."

Angelina led the way down to Deck Two and toward the bow. They approached a metal door. A plastic plaque with the words STAFF MESS emblazoned on it hung on the wall.

Angelina paused and keyed her radio.

"Bridge, this is Angelina. Do you copy?"

"We copy," answered Fletcher. "Everything's normal up here. We'll let you know if any alarms go off."

"Roger that." Angelina opened the door, ushering Tatyana, Giselle, and Nostradamus inside.

Tatyana closed her eyes and opened her senses, welcoming any spirits to contact her. She picked up no indications of current paranormal activity. Just a slight buzz as if there may have been something otherworldly here previously, more than likely the traces of Branden's soul.

"I'm not getting anything either."

Tatyana opened her eyes to see Nick standing by the door to the kitchen, leaning against the jamb. She checked on Nostradamus to see if he had picked up anything. The dog stood by a singed spot on the tiles, sniffing the area for a few seconds before moving away to rejoin Tatyana.

"That's the location where Brendan died," said Angelina.

"Are you getting anything?" asked Giselle.

"Nothing. Let me try the kitchen."

"I found nothing in there," offered Nick.

Tatyana entered and wandered around, followed by Giselle and Angelina. She paused by the stoves, ovens, and deep fryers to see if she could detect any supernatural auras. Nostradamus stayed beside her, more attracted by the smells of previously cooked meals than any paranormal entities. After five minutes, she gave up.

"I'm not sensing anything."

"I told you so," Nick added with a grin.

Tatyana flashed him an aggravated look out of the corner of her eye. "There's one more thing I'd like to try. Sometimes spirits remain dormant. Maybe I can summon them. If any are here, it should work."

"Be my guest," said Angelina.

Tatyana left the kitchen and stood in the center of the dining hall. She momentarily considered creating a circle of salt to protect the others but ruled it out. What she planned on was a shot in the dark. She doubted the ship contained paranormal energy.

"I'm calling on the spirit or spirits who reside aboard this ship. I want to talk with you."

Tatyana sensed no change in the spectral aura.

"To the spirit or spirits who reside here, please contact me. I mean you no harm. I only wish to talk."

Still nothing.

Tatyana wandered throughout the dining area and kitchen, occasionally pausing to repeat the incantations, each time with the same results. Nick stayed close by in the hopes of detecting anything she could not. Following each incantation, he shook his head. After forty-five minutes of trying, Tatyana gave up. Even Nostradamus had abandoned the effort, leaving her side twenty minutes ago to curl up beside the exit.

"Face it," said Nick. "There's nothing here."

Tatyana sighed. "You're probably right."

"Who's probably right?" asked Giselle.

"Sorry. I'm talking to myself."

"I assume there are no ghosts?" Giselle suggested, a tinge of hope in her tone.

"I don't think so, but I want to try one more thing if you don't mind."

"Go ahead. I want the results of the investigation to be conclusive."

Tatyana moved over to where Brendan had been incinerated and stood on the singed tiles. She took a deep breath to quell her nerves. She doubted this would work. If it did, she would call up a spiritual world of trouble.

"I'm calling on the spirit or spirits aboard this ship. Please talk to me."

Again, no change in the spectral aura.

"To the spirit or spirits residing here, please contact me. I mean you no harm. I only wish to know if you can tell me anything about this man's death."

Still nothing.

"If there are any spirits here, I demand you contact me. Show yourselves and make your presence known."

Giselle stepped back a few feet. Thankfully, as Tatyana had anticipated, nothing happened. She glanced over at Nick, who leaned against the wall by Nostradamus. He shook his head again. Tatyana agreed.

"I'm sorry, ladies. There is no paranormal activity on this ship."

Giselle smiled. "There's nothing to be sorry about. You did exactly what corporate asked."

Angelina did not seem convinced. "Are you sure?"

"Pretty sure."

"'Pretty sure'?" Giselle raised an eyebrow. "Corporate's going to want certainty."

"There's always a possibility that an entities or entities are present who refuse to make themselves known, but that's unlikely. We detected no signs of a paranormal aura here."

Angelina switched her gaze between Tatyana and Giselle. "We?"

"Me and Nostradamus."

"Good save," mouthed Nick.

"So, that's it then?" Giselle sounded extremely pleased. "Your conclusion is that there is no paranormal activity aboard this ship."

"Correct."

"Excellent. Let's go tell the captain."

✕　✕　✕

BACK ON THE bridge, Giselle informed Captain Fletcher they had no evidence of ghosts aboard the ship, then allowed Tatyana to relate the details of her investigation and findings.

Once the ladies finished, the captain pondered what he had heard.

"I guess that settles it," he finally said. "Thank you, Miss Reynolds. We've conclusively ruled out the possibility of ghosts being related to paranormal issues."

Paolo, the helmsman on duty the day of the incident, cleared his throat.

Fletcher turned to him. "Do you have something to add?"

"Sorry to disagree with you, sir, but I don't think we can conclusively rule out the possibility of paranormal activity."

"Why do you say that?"

"The incident with Mr. Sullivan occurred while we were at sea, but Miss Reynold's investigation was conducted while in port."

Giselle cut off Paolo. "I'm aware of that."

"We had no reports of strange occurrences aboard ship or any issues with the fire control system while docked. It's possible that whatever caused Mr. Sullivan's death occurred because we were underway."

"She does have a point," added Angelina. "The problem we had with the rudder would be something we'd only detect while at sea."

Fletcher turned to Tatyana. "Assuming the existence of ghosts on board, is it possible they could lay dormant while in port and become active once we set sail?"

Tatyana nodded. "It's not unusual for spirits to be aroused by certain circumstances."

"Correct me if I'm wrong, but we can't rule out the possibility of ghosts until you conduct the investigation again while we're at sea?"

"You're correct." Tatyana did not like where this was going.

"And that also holds true for possible system malfunctions that might occur while underway." Fletcher spoke it as a fact rather than a question. He stepped away from the others and moved to the windows along the front of the bridge, staring across the bow for a minute as he considered his next course of action. When the captain turned around and rejoined the rest of the party, he had determination in his eyes. "Miss Reynolds, if you conducted the same investigation at sea with the same results, could you say with certainty the ship is not haunted?"

"Yes."

"That also holds with the rudder control and fire detection systems," added Paolo.

"I think it's obvious what we have to do next."

Giselle grimaced. "You want to take the *Maria Doria* back out and conduct the paranormal investigation at sea."

"It's the only way we can present our findings to the board with any degree of certainty. Do you concur, Miss DeMarco?"

"Yes." Giselle sighed. "I was hoping to wrap this all up tonight."

"We all were," agreed the captain.

Tatyana hesitated before asking, "Do you still need me to conduct the investigation?"

Giselle forced a smile and nodded.

"At sea?"

"Yes."

Fletcher seemed confused. "Is anything wrong?"

"I never learned how to swim. The idea of a cruise in the middle of the Gulf of Mexico terrifies me."

The captain tried to sound as comforting as possible. "I can assure you, cruise liners today are among the safest modes of transportation around. Besides, we won't be traveling far. We'll stay close to shore the entire time in case we lose rudder control again."

"I don't know." Tatyana suppressed a shiver.

Giselle reached out and placed a gentle hand on Tatyana's shoulder. "We paid you to come here and conduct an investigation, and you fulfilled your part of the bargain."

"Thank you."

"I understand if you turn this down. And there are no hard feelings if you do. But it would mean a lot to me if you agreed."

"Because you don't want to pay someone else?" Tatyana joked.

"No. Because you're the best at what you do."

The last thing Tatyana wanted was to agree to this, but she realized she had no choice. Giselle had been upfront from the beginning, and Tatyana did not want to let her down, especially over something as ridiculous as her fear of drowning. Still, it's not easy to overcome one's phobias.

"How long will we be gone?"

"Twenty-four hours," responded Fletcher. "Give or take."

"When will you leave?"

"It'll take two days to call back the crew and prepare for departure, assuming we get permission to proceed."

"I'll get corporate to sign off on it by this afternoon," said Giselle.

"We'll shoot for a Monday evening departure. That will give us a chance to test the rudder before you conduct your investigation. If all goes well, we'll be back in port Tuesday afternoon."

Tatyana raised an eyebrow. "If all goes well?"

Fletcher smiled. "A figure of speech, ma'am. You're welcome to stay on board until then."

"Thank you."

"Is that alright with you?" asked Giselle.

Tatyana nodded. "It's fine. I'll call the university and let them know I've been delayed a few days." God knew it wouldn't be the first time she missed teaching classes to conduct paranormal activities.

The group went their separate ways. Angelina escorted Tatyana and Nostradamus back to her suite.

"Thank you for agreeing to conduct another investigation," offered Angelina with sincerity. "It means a lot to the captain."

"You're welcome. But I thought Giselle was the driving

force behind all this."

"She is, but Giselle views this from a corporate perspective. The board wants her to exhaust all possibilities to find out what caused the incident and correct it. Their interest is in protecting the brand name of Miami Cruise Lines and keeping the shareholders happy. Captain Fletcher sees things differently. This is his ship, and we're his family. The *Maria Doria* isn't like one of those mega-cruise liners with so many crew members the captain can't possibly know them all. He knows every crew member by name."

"Does he think there may be a paranormal explanation for this?"

"None of us do, to be honest. But the captain took the death of Brendan personally. He had known him for years and attended his wedding last fall in Atlanta. He wants to ensure we find what caused the accident and fix it so no one else gets hurt. That means he'll consider any possibility no matter how...." Angelina paused as she considered the right word.

"Bizarre?"

"Unlikely." They stopped at Tatyana's suite. "When you want breakfast, call down to room service. They open at 0700. Or you can leave the ship. There are dozens of places to eat near the port and downtown area."

Tatyana entered the suite. Nostradamus ran into the bedroom and dived onto the mattress, falling asleep in minutes.

As she expected, Nick waited for her on the sofa. "I'm proud of you."

"For what?"

"For agreeing to continue the investigation. I know how scared you are of doing this."

"How do you know that?"

"Remember, as a ghost, I can sense how you're feeling. I can empathize."

"But you loved your time at sea with the Navy. You were willing to return after you found Kathleen cheating on you."

"I probably would have made a career out of it if she hadn't murdered me." Nick stood and came over to Tatyana. "I knew a guy who enlisted at the same time I did. We became good friends. He was from Ohio and had never seen the ocean before. The poor guy was scared shitless on our first tour. I helped him through the first few days, and he eventually came to love the sea. I can do the same for you."

Tatyana nodded her head in appreciation. "What happened to your friend?"

"He was killed in a kamikaze attack off Okinawa."

"Not very helpful. Go somewhere. I need to get some sleep."

"Okay. See you tomorrow." Nick morphed into a mist and disappeared.

Tatyana entered the bedroom to the sound of snoring. Nostradamus lay across the king-size bed, hogging both sides, sound asleep. She changed into her nightclothes and slid under the covers, nudging the dog several times before he finally woke up, yawned, and scootched over to one side. Barely had she settled down when Nostradamus rolled over and snuggled beside his mistress, nearly pushing her off the bed. Tatyana didn't mind. Having him sleep next to her always took away her anxiety.

Tonight, she needed it.

CHAPTER SEVEN

TATYANA SLEPT IN until almost noon, partly because she was exhausted from the long day and partly because the gentle rocking of the ship in port proved quite soothing. Maybe she could get used to being at sea.

Since the WiFi did not work on the ship while passengers were not onboard and Nostradamus had to go for a walk anyway, Tatyana packed up her laptop and decided to go ashore for a while. She eventually found herself sitting outside an Internet café a few blocks inland from the river, sipping on a cappuccino while slowly working through a lemon poppy seed muffin. The waitress was kind enough to bring out a bowl of water for Nostradamus which, along with a nap, satisfied his cravings. Tatyana used this opportunity to conduct some research.

Other than discovering the *Maria Doria* was also the name of a sunken cruise liner that played a key role in the *Tomb Raider II* video game, there was little information about the ship other than the promotions of it on the Miami Cruise Lines website. She found numerous reviews of the liner's first shortened tour, all of them extremely unfavorable. Most of those ranted about how horrible the cruise was; none offered any helpful information on what had happened.

She switched her search to the crew members, most notably Captain Fletcher and Staff Captain Sullivan. Again, she found limited information on them, none of it negative. Fletcher had a stellar career spanning more than twenty years. His name appeared in a few reviews, all by passengers gushing over him.

Sullivan's name only appeared on the cruise line's website. A similar search on Giselle found only a few links, each connected to the corporate website.

This was proving as elusive as the supposed ghosts on the *Maria Doria*.

Tatyana thought for a few minutes and typed "Miami Cruise Lines" into the search bar. She received hits that filled thirty-eight pages. Each one pertained to booking a cruise. Refining her terms to include only news reports, this time she narrowed the field down to two pages. Scanning through them one at a time, she found nothing that raised any red flags. A few articles about the founding of the cruise line seven years ago. A *Wall Street Journal* piece about how Miami Cruise Lines dominated the market on inexpensive Caribbean trips. A *New Orleans CityBusiness* report on how one of the liner's cruise ships went out of commission suddenly. And three articles from local newspapers, including *The Advocate*, on the incident aboard the *Maria Doria*, none providing much in the way of details, the information having been filtered through corporate in Miami.

Typing in "ship accidents at sea" produced hundreds of results, mainly focusing on the *Titanic*, the *Lusitania*, and the *Andrea Doria*. Refining the search term to "ship fires at sea" received almost as many hits. Tatyana was amazed to discover three hundred and thirty-eight recorded incidents of fires aboard commercial and naval vessels in the past three centuries. When she narrowed the search to "ship fires near New Orleans," the only incident that came up involved the *S.S. Union Faith*, a Taiwanese freighter, that in 1969 collided with three barges carrying twenty-seven thousand barrels of crude oil, setting the freighter on fire and threatening to melt the Great New Orleans Bridge. Interesting, but nothing of use to her.

Giving up on her research, Tatyana paid for her meal. She was packing up to head back to the ship when her cell phone rang. The call came from Giselle.

"Hello, Giselle. What's up?"

"I stopped by your suite, but you weren't there."

"Afraid I skipped out?"

Giselle chuckled. "Yes, until I saw your luggage still in the room. I wanted to let you know that corporate approved our plan to take the *Maria Doria* to sea on Monday."

"Good." Tatyana only half meant it.

"They had a favor to ask. If it turns out that a ghost is aboard ship, would you be willing to exorcise it?"

"First, an exorcism is for demonic possession. If the *Maria Doria* is possessed, I'm not qualified to handle it. I do spiritual cleansings. The problem is, I didn't bring any of the things I need to perform one."

"How difficult would it be to get hold of them?"

Tatyana paused a moment to think about it. Giselle mistook the silence for hesitation.

"Corporate is willing to pay you an extra $50,000 if you perform an exor.... a cleansing."

"Are you serious?"

"Corporate is desperate to clear this up and get the ship back in service so we don't have to cancel another tour. What do you need?"

"I'm sure I can get everything I need downtown. That won't be a problem."

Giselle sounded excited. "Get whatever you need and keep the receipts. We'll reimburse you."

"Deal."

"Thank you so much. I'll let the board know you agreed. Chat later."

The line went dead. Tatyana slid the phone into her back pocket. She called to Nostradamus, who raised his head and wagged his tail.

"It looks like I'll be going into town tonight."

The dog barked and broke into a smile. Tatyana gathered her belongings and headed back to the ship, taking the long way so Nostradamus could do his business.

×　×　×

EARLY THAT EVENING, Tatyana walked down to Bourbon Street to experience the nightlife in New Orleans. She ate dinner at Mambo's Creole Restaurant. The food was fantastic and flavorful, but a bit spicey for an old New England gal like herself. She considered bringing the leftovers back to the ship for Nostradamus but decided against it, afraid of what it might do to his digestive system. The last thing she wanted was to be cleaning up his mess all night.

Tatyana followed dinner with a two-hour walking tour of ghost and vampire spots in the French Quarter. She did not do it for the paranormal aspect. Nothing the guide could have shown her could compare to what she had experienced over the last year. However, it did give her a chance to tour the French Quarter, learn a little about the city, and experience the wonders first-hand. The aromas of spicey food. The sounds of people enjoying themselves and jazz bands playing. The vibrancy of the city. Nothing Dartmouth offered could match this.

One thing that did catch Tatyana's interest was a shop they passed on Conti Street named Paranormal Emporium. When the tour ended, she returned to the shop, hoping it would have what she needed to perform a cleansing ritual.

A bell sounded as Tatyana entered. The shop itself extended deep into the back, making it appear much larger than it seemed from the street. Soft jazz played over speakers mounted in the corners near the ceiling. A minty fragrance filtered through the building, one quite familiar to Tatyana—sage. T-shirts and gifts dominated the front of the store, catering to the thousands of tourists who passed through New Orleans. Most of the shirts were overpriced, bearing the store logo or various views of New Orleans with spectral images. The souvenirs were

SCOTT M. BAKER

cheap, designed to attract people who wanted to spend money on an inexpensive souvenir. A small bookshelf centered against one wall contained used copies of novels, mainly by Anne Rice, or contemporary histories defining vampirism in the city, ghost stories of New Orleans and the south, and other related books.

Tatyana made her way into the back where she found tables filled with items geared toward those whose interests tended more toward the supernatural. Stones and crystals of every color, including Selenite, Bloodstone, Sodalite, Amazonite, Lapis Lazuli, Clear Quartz, Chrysocolla, and Black Tourmaline. Candles. Bells. Sage sticks of various sizes and. Home-made jewelry containing crystals. Tarot and oracle cards. Altar dressings. And other related trinkets.

"May I help you?"

The voice startled Tatyana. She glanced around until she saw an older woman standing behind the counter. The beads on the doorway behind her still swayed, so she must have entered from the rear of the building. Tatyana guessed she was in her late seventies but could easily be off by a decade considering the woman's appearance. Age lines deeply creased her tanned face and hands, and her frizzy hair had long since turned white. She wore a shabby yellow dress at least twenty years old with a brown wool shawl draped over her shoulders and upper arms. The older woman shuffled from behind the counter, her hands shaking. Despite her age, she focused her gaze on Tatyana with a pair of piercing blue eyes that still beamed with vitality.

"I'm sorry to have startled you, *chère*. I have a tendency to sneak up on people."

"It's my fault. I was busy browsing." Tatyana stepped over and bowed slightly. "I'm Tatyana.

"Adelaide. It's not often I get people in this part of my store."

"You have an excellent selection. And your prices are reasonable."

52

"Unlike up front?"

Tatyana grew embarrassed. "I didn't mean to imply—"

Adelaide laughed. "No offense taken. This is my passion, supplying those interested in the spiritual world. I have a small but loyal clientele, but their business doesn't pay the bills. That's why I sell overpriced souvenirs to *le gogo*." Her face broke into a toothless smile. "You take your time, *chère*. I'll be in back making something to drink. Call me when you're finished."

Tatyana spent the next half hour gathering what she needed in case a cleansing was necessary—thirty Selenite crystals, a score of sage candles, and a dozen containers of kosher salt. With everything placed on the back counter, she realized how much she intended to purchase and included an over-priced, gawdy travel bag in bright red with New Orleans embroidered on the side in gold stitching.

"Adelaide, I'm ready to check out."

The old woman shuffled out from behind the beaded curtain with two mugs of steaming tea. "I brought you a drink. Green tea. It's good for the body."

"Thank you." Tatyana blew on it and then took a long sip. Her eyes lit up as the tea slid down her throat. "What's in that?"

"Kentucky bourbon, *chère*." Adelaide grinned. "That's what keeps you young."

The two women chatted amicably as Adelaide rang up the sale. Tatyana spent more than she usually did, but it didn't matter since Miami Cruise Lines was paying for it. As Tatyana packed her supplies, Adelaide handed her a receipt.

"*Chère*, may I ask you a question?"

"Of course."

"What do you plan on doing with all this?"

"I'm a paranormal investigator."

Adelaide nodded. "I should have known. Most customers come in looking for crystals and incense for holistic reasons.

Not you. You're gearing up to drive away ghosts."

"Did you used to be a paranormal investigator?"

"When I was young. Many years ago." Adelaide took a long sip of her spiked tea. "Back then, we called ourselves ghost hunters or Forteans. Those were good days. And do I have stories to tell. As I'm sure you do. I planned on boring my grandchildren with them. Sadly, I never had none."

"It's an exciting life."

"It is. But it's also a risky one, *chère*." Adelaide clasped Tatyana's hand. "I don't know what you're planning on doing, but you're in danger."

The warning caught Tatyana by surprise. "How do you know that?"

"There's a dreadful aura about you."

"You mean something has attached itself to me?"

Adelaide shook her head. "No. But wherever you've been, it tainted you. Like a non-smoker who sits at a bar for too long, the smell lingers. It's the same with the ghosts you're dealing with."

"I was at a site that was supposedly haunted but didn't detect anything."

"Because they didn't want to make themselves known. Trust me, *chère*. These ghosts have already been aroused once, and the results cost someone their life."

Tatyana stared at Adelaide, dumbfounded. "How did you know that?"

"*Chère*, when you've been doing this as long as I have, you become uncomfortably attuned to the spirit world. Most of the time I ignore it, like background noise when you ride the bus. But every once in a while, there's a psychic scream you can't ignore. I experienced one several weeks ago. It occurred not too far from here. The pain and anger of numerous tormented souls crying out."

"There's more than one?"

Adelaide closed her eyes. For the first time, the older woman seemed disturbed by the paranormal.

"How many?"

"That I don't know. All I can tell you is that if you continue with this, I can't guarantee you'll live."

"Is that a premonition?"

"A sixth sense."

Which is precisely what Nick had told her. "Do you know how… I mean, if I don't…? Do you know how I'll die?"

"Sorry, but no." Adelaide reached out and clasped Tatyana's hand. "I can offer you a Tarot reading. That might provide an answer."

The thought of knowing the possible future terrified Tatyana. "Thank you, but I'll pass."

Tatyana gathered her new travel bag, thanked Adelaide, and rushed out of the shop, where she hailed a taxi back to port.

✕　✕　✕

TATYANA HAD THE taxi driver let her out in front of a bar across the street from the port. The word Sazerac blazed in blue from the neon sign hanging in the window. After her earlier conversation with Nick and tonight's warning from Adelaide, she needed a drink to help calm her nerves. Paying the driver and passing him a generous tip, Tatyana climbed out, hefted the gawdy travel bag over her shoulder, and went in.

The inside had a quaint feeling to it. Tatyana could tell the establishment had been around for a while due to the exposed wooden beams supporting the ceiling and the slightly-tarnished mahogany back bar behind the cocktail station, with a hutch that dominated the wall with two small and one large arch above the shelves and a wide mirror in the center. Over a hundred bottles of every type and brand of alcohol filled the shelves. Antiques from New Orleans' history covered the walls and soft jazz played through the ceiling-mounted speakers. Despite the pleasant ambiance, only a handful of customers were around, which suited Tatyana. She needed a quiet place to relax.

Tatyana sat where the bar made an L turn and connected with the wall. Three seats were arranged along this portion. She sat at the center one and placed her bag on the seat to the right so no one would bother her.

A few seconds later, the bartender approached, an attractive woman with aqua-colored hair, a ruby stud in her nose, and tattoos along her arms and chest. She broke into a smile half friendly, half flirtatious.

"I'm Veronica. My friends call me Roni. You can call me anything you like. What can I get you?"

"I need a drink bad. Do you have Merlot?"

Veronica leaned over the bar and whispered conspiratorially. "The wine here sucks. The owner buys the cheapest shit he can find. I don't know why you need a drink, but whatever the reason, forget the wine. Liquor is quicker."

"I don't usually drink hard stuff. What do you recommend?"

"I have just the drink for a pretty young thing like you." Veronica grabbed a metal shaker from the bar and began pouring various alcohols into it. "I hope you don't mind my being nosy, but are you having guy troubles?"

"Problems at work." It wasn't the truth, but neither was it a lie.

"I hear you. I hated putting in a forty-hour-a-week prison sentence in a cubicle stuck in a dingy office. Now I work here, and it's awesome."

"At least it's quiet."

"Tonight, yeah, because there are no cruise ships. When one pulls in for a port call, this place is packed with crew members blowing off steam. And when a ship returns to port, we get a lot of tourists who come in here to continue partying as long as they can. They leave the best tips because they're drunk, happy, and have money. What do you do for a living?"

"I cleanse buildings of unwanted things."

"You do pest control?"

Tatyana never thought of that way, but the description fit. "Sort of."

"I never would have pegged you for an exterminator."

"Why?"

"You're too pretty."

Veronica finished her concoction, placed the lid on the shaker, and mixed it with enough fervor that her boobs noticeably bounced, all the while eyeing Tatyana. When finished, Veronica half-filled a tumbler with ice, poured the drink, and then placed the glass in front of Tatyana. It had a reddish-amber color and smelled powerful.

"What is it?" Tatyana asked.

"Try it first and see if you like it."

Tatyana raised the tumbler and took a drink. A hint of black licorice caressed her tongue. Veronica had put a lot of alcohol in it. Tatyana felt a slight yet pleasant burning sensation as the drink slid down her throat. Damn, it was good. She smiled despite herself.

"I knew you'd like it."

Tatyana took another sip. "What is it?"

"It's a New Orleans version of an Old Fashioned. We call it a Sazerac. It was created here in the 1830s. It was originally made with Cognac until insects destroyed the Cognac grapes in France, so we switched to rye whiskey, which we have a lot of here. It has bitters from a Haitian family recipe, a splash of absinthe, and is garnished with a lemon peel."

"It's good."

"I'm glad you like it. The first one is on the house."

"Thank you." Tatyana took her third sip. "I'll definitely want a second."

"You got it, sexy."

Veronica made a second drink as Tatyana nursed along the first. She waited on a few other customers, then returned to Tatyana with the drink and slid it in front of her.

"So, what's eating you?"

"What do you mean?" Tatyana finished off the first drink and slid the empty tumbler aside.

"I've been doing this long enough to know when something is bothering my customers. I'm here if you want to talk."

Tatyana thought about it. Maybe talking with someone impartial might do some good.

"I'll tell you, but you won't believe me."

"I've spent eight years in this bar chatting up people. Try me."

Tatyana grabbed the second tumbler and swigged some Sazerac. "I'm a paranormal investigator. My client has asked me to investigate a death that recently took place that has no logical explanation."

"You're talking about the guy who died aboard the *Maria Doria* a few weeks ago."

"How did you know that?"

Veronica chuckled. "The only thing that spreads faster than rumors in the cruise industry is STDs. Plus, if you were staying at a hotel, you'd be in one of the nicer bars downtown. You're here in this dive, so you're probably staying on one of the ships."

"Damn, you're good."

"Tell me something I don't know," Veronica replied flirtatiously. She took a cherry from a glass on the bar, seductively slid it along her lips, and used her tongue to suck it into her mouth. "But go on."

"Long story short, I couldn't detect anything aboard the ship, so I couldn't perform a spectral cleansing. Now they want to take the ship to sea, hoping the entities will show themselves there. I've had two people with psychic abilities warn me that if I go on this voyage, I may not come back."

"Are you scared?"

"God, yes. I'm terrified of water."

"I meant of ghosts."

"No."

"Then what's bothering you?"

Tatyana thought about that question for a few seconds. "I've dealt with a few evil spirits before. I'll admit, it was scary at the time, but I sent them to the afterlife. I'm used to dealing with them by now, malevolent and otherwise. These premonitions of something bad happening have shaken my confidence."

"Let me ask you something. Are you doing this job for a loved one or a close friend?"

"No."

"Are you doing this to help out someone? Like exorcising someone's house of a dangerous ghost or getting rid of something attached to a person?"

"No."

"Are you doing this to clean a public place, like a school or hospital, to make it safe?"

Tatyana shook her head.

"Who benefits from this?"

"Miami Cruise Lines."

"There you go." Veronica tapped Tatyana's hand three times, letting her palm rest on it when done. "You need to ask yourself if your life is worth what's being asked of you."

"That puts it into perspective."

"I told you I'm good." Veronica winked at Tatyana, then pushed the tumbler of Sazerac closer to her. "You finish this while I make you a third. This one's on me. But you have to tell me some of your ghost stories."

✕ ✕ ✕

TATYANA STAGGERED HER way back to the cruise liner.

Veronica had made that third drink stronger than the first two, which didn't bother her. Tatyana had nursed it along as she shared paranormal tales with the bartender. An hour later, she said goodbye, leaving the bar with a better appreciation of her situation, a buzz, and Veronica's phone number. By the time she reached her quarters, she was ready for a good sleep.

Entering the suite, Tatyana was disappointed that Nick was not waiting for her as he usually did. Figures. The one time she wanted him to drop by and annoy her, he chose to stay away. She wanted to discuss with him her trepidation about continuing with this job and get his opinion. Oh, well. She knew he'd be around sooner or later. Besides, considering how much she had drank, it would probably be better if she went to bed and slept it off.

As she placed the travel bag beside the sofa, she noticed a note on the coffee table from one of the crew noting that he had taken Nostradamus for a walk. Thank God. She doubted she could make it back down to the dock.

Entering the bedroom, she found the Pitbull curled up on the bed, hogging the pillows. Nostradamus lifted his head, wagged his tail upon seeing her, then went back to sleep.

Tatyana kicked off her shoes. She would undress and shower in the morning. Climbing into bed, she yanked a pillow from underneath Nostradamus' head for her own use. His eyes never opened, though his tail wagged again. Tatyana pulled what she could of the comforter over her, cuddled close to the dog, and fell asleep.

CHAPTER EIGHT

THE EXCEPTIONALLY BRIGHT light roused Tatyana from her slumber. That, and the loud snoring. She knew the latter came from Nostradamus. He often woke her up in the middle of the night. But she had no clue where the light came from. Rolling over, it caused her to squint. Tatyana shaded her eyes with her arm. Sunlight blazed through the cabin windows. She rolled over and placed a pillow on her head. Crap, how long had she been asleep?

Not long enough, apparently. Her head throbbed, her stomach ached, and her mouth felt furrier than Nostradamus' back. Now she remembered why she hadn't drank that much since she was an undergraduate. And last night, she only had three drinks. What a lightweight she had become.

Tatyana slowly crawled out of bed to limit the pounding behind her eyes. Nostradamus raised his head, stared at her, and nodded off. Once the pain subsided, she made her way out of the bedroom and into the suite.

"It's about time you woke up."

Now Nick shows up. "Don't be so loud. Besides, it's still morning."

Nick laughed from his seat on the sofa. "It's after noon."

She glanced at her watch. It read 12:21. Damn. She wasted half the day. Not that she could do much in her condition.

Tatyana went over to the kitchenette and poured herself a drink of water. "You must enjoy seeing me like this."

"On the contrary. I sympathize." Nick pushed himself off the sofa and joined her. "I had more than my fair share of shore leave experiences. One night in Honolulu, I went on a bender after having lived through a *kamikaze* attack off Leyte. A bunch of my shipmates had to drag me back to the ship. I don't remember most of that night, and my friends would never tell me what happened. But we were banned from the bar."

"That's supposed to make me feel better?"

"Not really. I just wanted to remind you that you're not the first person to wake up with a hangover."

"Thanks." Tatyana took a long drink of water, not stopping until the parch in her throat was satiated. She had finished two-thirds of the glass.

Nick leaned against the wall. "Since we're not setting sail until tomorrow, what's on the agenda for today? Or what's left of it."

"Funny." Tatyana rolled her eyes. She refilled her glass and brought it into the suite, taking a seat on the love seat by the window. "I need to ask you something."

"Go ahead." Nick sat on the opposite sofa.

Tatyana stared into her glass for a few seconds, summoning the nerve to express her thoughts. "What would you think if I declined to go tomorrow? I mean, what would you think of me?"

"I wouldn't think any different of you. Why do you ask?"

"I fulfilled my obligation to the company. There are no spirits aboard this ship."

"Are you sure? The crew thinks they won't show themselves until we're underway."

"If there were any on board, we'd feel them. Right?"

"Unless they were purposefully concealing themselves." Nick focused his gaze on Tatyana.

Tatyana shrugged. "Maybe."

"Are you afraid to go to sea?"

"Being on a cruise ship in the middle of the ocean is not my idea of fun, but I'll do it if I had to."

"Then what's bothering you?"

Tatyana sighed. "Remember how you said you had a bad feeling about the ship?"

"Yeah?"

"Last night, while picking up supplies, I met a psychic who said the same thing. She claimed I had an aura around me that boded ill."

"Do you believe her?"

"I believe *you*. She confirmed what you sensed." Tatyana stood and made her way over to the window, staring off into the Mississippi. "Is this worth it?"

"You mean cleansing the ship?"

Tatyana nodded. "Assuming there are any. You remember back in Salem when we fought Eliza Adams, and what happened to Denholm Goss? If there's an entity aboard the *Maria Doria*, it killed the staff captain for no reason. That's a level of malevolence we've not encountered before. Is it worth putting our lives at risk?"

"My life isn't at risk."

"You know what I mean." Tatyana turned to face Nick. "It's not like I'm cleansing a spirit from a home or an entity that attached itself to someone. I'm risking my life so a cruise company can make money."

"I understand." Nick did not sound convincing.

"There's a 'but' in your voice."

"You know me too well." Nick smiled. "Look at it from the ghost's point of view."

Tatyana stepped away from the window and sat down. "You lost me."

"Take Eliza, for example. I'm not excusing her actions, but she had a good reason to hate Denholm. Suppose whatever killed the staff captain had a reason for its actions? Cleansing it might release the entity, allowing it to continue to its afterlife, even if it's to Hell."

"Is that worth getting killed over?"

"For you, maybe not." Nick shrugged. "But when you

cleansed Kathleen, you released Gabriella and her parents from captivity. As well as Mrs. Wells, Mr. Dobbs, and Cheryl."

Tatyana said nothing.

"And me."

"Alright, you made your point." Tatyana took a long drink of water.

Nick leaned forward and rested his elbows on his knees. "I'm not dismissing your concerns. I remember Eliza. She was the most dangerous ghost we've dealt with so far. She kicked our asses. And if my sixth sense is right, we're facing something just as bad now. But we have no idea what we're dealing with. We should figure out what we're facing before we decide whether or not to do anything about it."

"Agreed." Tatyana hesitated. "But that doesn't mean I'm not concerned about what will happen once we leave port."

"I wish I could help. Though I know someone who might be able to."

"Who?"

"That psychic you met."

CHAPTER NINE

TATYANA STOOD ACROSS the street from the Paranormal Emporium, trying to decide whether to go in. The shop closed at nine. It was already ten of. If she intended to do this, she needed to act now.

Her inaction had nothing to do with disbelief in Tarot readings. The ability to predict the future was another aspect of being attuned to the spiritual world. Tatyana's concern centered around whether Adelaide could conduct a legitimate reading, or did she merely claim to be able to dupe tourists. Knowing what the future held, especially if the outcome proved bad, would be difficult enough, but at least Tatyana could be prepared for the worse. If Adelaide turned out to be a charlatan, taking on the spirit with inaccurate information would not end well. She had earlier reasoned that being prepared was better than going in blind, no matter the outcome. Now she had second thoughts.

After contemplating for another five minutes, Tatyana decided to go for it. Taking a deep breath to steady her nerves, she crossed Conti Street and entered the store.

The bell on the door rang as she entered. Adelaide called out from the back room.

"Sorry, we're about to close. If you want anything, you'll have to make it...." Adelaide stepped between the beaded curtain, her face lighting up on seeing Tatyana. "I had a feeling you'd be back."

Tatyana hesitantly walked up to the rear counter. "I've been thinking about what you said last night, about there being a bad aura surrounding me."

"The word I used was dreadful. *Chère*, we walk in the same spiritual realm. I talk to the dead. You release them from their earthly bonds. I can sense the apprehension in you. You're scared because you don't know what you might encounter. Am I right?"

"Yes."

"And you're here because you're hoping a Tarot reading may give you a clue as to what to expect if you attempt to contact this spirit."

So much for considering Adelaide a fraud. "Yes."

"I'll do a reading for you, *chère*. But let me warn you, I don't sugarcoat things. I'm not the type to tell someone they'll find love, happiness, and wealth if that's not what the cards show. Are you certain you want to continue?"

Every ounce of common sense told Tatyana to decline, hit Sazerac one more time, then go back to the *Maria Doria* and pack.

When did she ever listen to common sense?

"Yes. Let's do a reading."

Adelaide nodded and patted Tatyana on the hand. She came around the counter, made her way to the door, locked it, and turned the plastic sign around so the CLOSED portion faced out. Returning to the counter, she shut off the lights and then pushed through the beaded curtains into the back, motioning for Tatyana to follow.

The reading room could have been set up by a Hollywood set designer. An oval, wooden table covered with a red velvet cloth and maroon winged-back chairs dominated the center of the room. A Victorian-style tiffany lamp sat to the left, casting the table in a mellow glow. The walls were painted a bright cherry red. White mini-Christmas lights hung where the walls met the ceiling and along the support beams. An antique dresser rested along the right wall and, directly above it, a French Victorian Giltwood Girandole mirror with lit candles in the twin candelabras. Off to its right sat a display case containing ten wooden boxes bearing artwork in different styles, from modern and abstract to richly-detailed classic images. The only other decorations in the room were six faux bronze frames containing graphics of some of the symbols of positive energy—the Ankh, the Pentagram, the Triquetra, the Eternal Knot, the Bagua, and the Toros.

Adelaide pulled red silk curtains across the beaded opening, headed for the display case, removed one of the boxes, and sat in the chair facing the front of the store. She gestured for Tatyana to sit opposite her. The lid bore the symbol for the Flower of Life carved into the surface and hi-lighted with gold leaf. Adelaide lifted the lid, revealing the Tarot cards resting inside. "Have you ever had a reading before?"

"This is my first time," Tatyana replied, a hint of embarrassment in her voice. "I don't know anything about Tarot decks."

"That's more common than you think. Usually, I allow those having their futures read to pick the deck they want to use. It makes them feel more in control. However, in this situation, I want to use the Arcana Cards. They indicate forces you have no control over which, in this instance, seems appropriate."

Adelaide placed the box inside a circle of crystal points between two flickering candles, one black and the other white. Opening the ornate lid, she removed the deck and moved the box off to the side, then shuffled overhand, sliding small groups of cards from one hand to the other. When finished, she offered the deck to Tatyana.

"These are from the major arcana, consisting of fifty-six cards in four suits representing different aspects of the actions and influences involved. What is read here has nothing to do with your actions or behavior but is deemed inevitable. Hold the cards and focus on the situation you're dealing with. If you feel compelled to cut and rearrange the cards, follow your intuition."

"What I need to know is—"

Adelaide raised her hand. "The Tarot already understands your concerns. I don't need to know them. Concentrate on the question you have for the cards. The cards will speak for themselves. Nothing is said out loud. Blind readings are the best practice."

A sense of foreboding filled Tatyana as she feared what the cards might tell her. Fighting the urge to leave, she steeled herself and focused on finding answers. Tatyana rearranged the cards, cutting and shuffling as Adelaide had done. Somehow the cards felt right. With a will of their own, they were ready to reveal their secrets. Tatyana placed the deck on the table.

Adelaide removed the top card and placed it down in the center of the crystals. It depicted an image of a young woman sitting on a rock by a lake, holding a sword above her head.

"This is a signifier card. It represents you. This one is the Page of Swords. It indicates a person who is intelligent and driven but does not have the life experiences of others around them. Most of the other signifier cards tend to focus on intelligent individuals who are innocent in their thinking or not emotionally grounded."

Tatyana nodded, taking it as a compliment.

Adelaide placed the next five cards face down around the signifier card at the points of an imaginary pentagram, then set the remainder of the deck to one side. She rested her fingers on the card in the lower left corner.

"This card represents the past." Adelaide flipped it face up.

The image showed six red-colored swords embedded in the ground. Above it was a rowboat operated by a blindfolded oarsman ferrying two skeletons. The card was inverted, facing away from Adelaide.

"This is the Six of Swords. Usually, it means calming waters are ahead of you. However, being reversed, it represents trouble in your future." Adelaide glanced up at Tatyana.

"Didn't you say you were investigating the haunting of the *Maria Doria?*"

"Yes."

"Then this card makes sense. In Tarot, the suit of Swords is associated with the element of air and usually deals with your mind in the present or the thoughts you currently possess. They also can be associated with conflict and strife. Are you going through any personal or professional turmoil at the moment?"

"Just uncertainty about what I'm dealing with on this assignment."

"Then this indicates something bad is not too far away. This suit's strengths are all in the realm of thought, intelligence, and communication. People connected to the suit of swords are curious, logical, disciplined, moral, and fair. However, the suit of swords can also be problematic. Swords can be used for good and evil, to save or hurt someone. Because of this, the suit of Swords is associated with conflict, aggression, and violence. When reversed, as in this case, Swords usually have to do with feelings of cruelty, sadness, and confusion."

Adelaide moved her hand to the upper right corner of the star. "This card represents the present."

She flipped it face up. The card displayed a skeleton lying on its back with ten red-colored swords piercing its ribcage, pelvis, and legs, the tips embedded in the ground. This card was also inverted.

"The Ten of Swords."

"That doesn't look good," said Tatyana.

"It isn't. When upright, the card signifies betrayal, deep wounds, and heavy loss. Being reversed, it represents a major disaster. Whatever the force is behind all of this, it's one of extreme magnitude, and you can't avoid it."

Adelaide shifted her hand across the star to the card on the upper left. "This one represents the problem you currently face."

She turned it over, revealing an image of a young woman

bowing. The woman clutched a sword in her right hand and had eight more embedded in her back.

"It's the Nine of Swords. It's symbolic of intensively negative emotions and an inability to cope with your current situation."

"What type of negative emotions?"

"It could be any of them. Fear, anxiety, anger, despair, guilt, regret, remorse, and revenge. Do you feel any of these?"

"No."

"Then the spirits you are dealing with do."

Adelaide moved her hand over to the card at the lower right. "This card will show you what you need to overcome the problem."

Adelaide turned it over.

It showed the skeleton of a creature with wings and a ram-like skull hovering above a doorway. The bottom of the card displayed a fiery background with two skulls on either side. Above the figure sat an inverted pentagram.

"What does that mean?" Tatyana leaned in, peering down at the card.

"It's the Devil card. It signifies the situation is out of your control. Let me ask you a question, and be honest. Do you feel you're in control of your behavior? Or are you obsessive, impulsive, or overly concerned with material things?"

"I've always considered myself well grounded."

"That's what I was afraid of. This indicates that the entities you're dealing with are outside your control. In light of the other three cards, this is a warning that there's considerable trouble ahead for you and that what happens may likely be beyond your ability to handle."

Tatyana attempted to lighten the mood. "You're not filling me with a lot of confidence."

"The cards only relate the truth." Adelaide reached up to the card at the top of the star and paused. "This one forewarns what the outcome of your venture will be. Are you ready?"

Tatyana hesitated in answering. She had come to Adelaide hoping to better understand whether the *Maria Doria* was haunted and heard more than she had bargained for. Every card painted a picture of a deadly and enraged entity that she might not be able to control.

"What happens if you don't turn the card over?"

"If you're asking if the outcome will be any different, the answer is no. You need to ask whether you want to know what the future holds."

Tatyana was not sure how to answer. Would knowing what the outcome might be, especially if disastrous, undermine her confidence to proceed with the cleansing? Probably. Would not knowing put her at a disadvantage? Definitely. A part of Tatyana urged her not to see the final card. However, Tatyana's rational side told her that being aware of what she might face would give her the best advantage.

She took a deep breath and nodded. "Turn it over."

Adelaide did.

The card that sat in front of them showed a tower spanning its length. Flames erupted from the center of the structure. Two lightning bolts struck the top of the tower, breaking off the tip, which crumbled to one side. The concern that flashed across Adelaide's face warned Tatyana this part of the reading would not be good.

"I assume that's bad news?"

"It couldn't get much worse, *chère*." Adelaide's voice had a slight waver to it. "This is The Tower card. It signifies disaster, chaos, and tragedy. According to the cards, whatever you're involved in will end in violence and death. If this card had appeared anywhere else in the reading, it would have signified a massive upheaval earlier in your life. In this case, it represents the future, so it's a warning that what you're about to engage in is a highly dangerous situation beyond your control." Adelaide sat back in her chair. "I'm sorry."

Tatyana sat dumbfounded, too stunned by what the reading had said to respond. She had no reason to doubt what Adelaide had told her. After all, Tatyana was a paranormal investigator and put as much faith in Tarot cards as she did in her own abilities. Still, that did not negate the fact the reading boded ill. Tatyana laughed sarcastically to herself. Boding ill was an understatement. Adelaide's reading foretold that Tatyana would be involved in a paranormal nightmare if she attempted to proceed with this cleansing.

Adelaide reached out and gently placed her fingers on Tatyana's hand. "I know this is a lot to take in, *chère*."

"Is there a chance that the reading may be…?"

"Wrong?"

Tatyana nodded her head, embarrassed over questioning the reader's integrity.

"It's okay. I take no offense at your question. And the answer is no, at least as far as I'm aware. No one has ever come back to complain that my reading was off. Sometimes there are slight variations to the results, but those are usually affected by changes in the lifestyle or choices of those who received the reading."

"I can avoid that future," Tatyana motioned toward the Tarot deck, "by altering the actions I take?"

"Of course. However, in this situation, you can only avoid the outcome predicted by the cards by not going through with the cleansing."

"But that would mean…." Tatyana could not bring herself to finish.

Adelaide nodded. "That would mean either leaving any souls trapped aboard the ship to suffer or stepping aside and letting someone else conduct the cleansing. Only they won't have the foresight of what's about to happen that you do. You have a tough decision to make."

An understatement, thought Tatyana, yet an accurate one.

Tatyana stood. "Thank you so much. I have to be going."

Adelaide remained seated. "Are you okay? Do you want to

talk?"

"No, but thank you. I haven't decided yet whether I'll go through with this."

Adelaide smiled and patted the top of Tatyana's closed hand. "*Chère*, we both know you'll do what's right, not what's convenient."

Adelaide escorted Tatyana to the front and unlocked the door. As Tatyana left, Adelaide placed a hand on her arm.

"I wish you the best, *chère*. I'll ask the spirit world to look after you."

Adelaide closed and locked the door, waved goodbye to Tatyana, and closed the curtains.

Tatyana headed back to the *Maria Doria*, trying to comprehend everything that had just occurred.

CHAPTER TEN

TATYANA STOOD ON the balcony of her suite, watching the river traffic along the Mississippi. Nostradamus curled up in a ball on the bed, his gaze fixed on his mistress, picking up on her distress. Tatyana appreciated that. Nostradamus was more than a dog. He was a great companion, a good detector of paranormal presences, as well as her protector. The last thing she wanted would be to put him in danger.

That was the problem with this entire situation. No matter what decision Tatyana made, someone—either herself or those on the ship—would be in danger.

I'm blowing this whole thing out of proportion, Tatyana reasoned. We haven't even determined if the liner contains a trapped soul. Their first attempt at a cleansing yesterday had been a bust. Neither her, Nick, or Nostradamus had detected any signs of a spectral presence. If there had been an aura, at least one of them would have picked up on it. The more she thought about it, the more the evidence pointed to a freak accident that could not be explained. Corporate pushed Giselle to explore all aspects of the paranormal realm merely so they could claim they had investigated everything. Tonight's cleaning would most likely be as unproductive.

If that were the case, why did a part of her want to throw away the money and get off the ship before it set sail?

Simple. Despite what the evidence and common sense suggested, Tatyana had enough faith in the spiritual world to accept what the Tarot cards had predicted. If she believed what the reading said, she also had to believe that going through with tonight's ritual would not end well. That is why Tatyana had already packed her luggage and stood on the balcony trying to decide whether to leave now and head back to New Hampshire or continue with this insanity.

Who am I kidding? She would never walk away. That was not her style. If a spirit is trapped aboard this ship, she could not allow it to suffer in this realm when she had an opportunity to set it free. And if it was evil, as Adelaide had suggested, it had to be exorcised. She had committed herself to doing this. Walking away was not an option she could live with. Either someone else would be called in to perform the cleansing and be caught off guard, possibly being hurt or worse. Or the company would ignore the situation and let this continue until another crew member or members were killed. Tatyana could not live with that on her conscience.

Tatyana allowed herself a small smile. Adelaide knew more about Tatyana than Tatyana did about herself.

A knock sounded on the door. Tatyana stepped back into the suite and yelled, "It's open."

A junior officer stepped into the suite. "Miss Reynolds, Captain Fletcher asked me to get you. We'll be pulling away from the dock in fifteen minutes."

✕   ✕   ✕

THE BRIDGE BUSTLED with activity when Tatyana and Nostradamus entered. Fletcher stood in front of the ECDIS console, reading through papers attached to a clipboard. Three other officers were behind the console. Angelina had the helm. Two other officers who she had not met before manned radar and communications. Giselle had positioned herself in the corner of the bridge overlooking the dock so she would be out of the way. Tatyana noticed that despite the nature of this voyage, the woman still wore a skirt and matching blazer, a red silk blouse, and black heels. Nick was also present, standing by the port bridge window overlooking the river. He waved as she entered but did not join her. Nostradamus left Tatyana's side and sat by his spectral friend.

Fletcher looked up as they entered. "Miss Reynolds, thank you for joining us."

"That's what I'm here for."

"We'll be setting sail once the harbor pilot is aboard. In the meantime, let me introduce you to the bridge crew. You already know Miss Rosario."

Angelina turned and waved.

"This is Mr. Campbell."

The tall, handsome Jamaican officer manning the radar offered Tatyana his hand. "It's a pleasure, ma'am."

"And this is Miss Hashimoto."

The young woman on communications smiled and bowed slightly.

"How many crew members are on board tonight?" asked Tatyana.

"Just the operating crew," answered Fletcher. "Navigation, engineering, propulsion, and maintenance. Approximately fifty people. There's no need for more."

A commotion behind them distracted Fletcher. He excused himself and greeted the harbor pilot who had been escorted onto the bridge. The captain clasped his hand.

"Jackson, good to see you. It's been a long time."

"I've been on vacation. Took the wife on a trip to Europe. Believe it or not, we took a Viking cruise of the Rhine. At least I didn't have to do any of the work."

Fletcher laughed. "The tugs are in place and ready when you are."

"Let's do this."

The captain nodded and announced, "Take her out."

Tatyana joined Nick and Nostradamus by the port windows as the forward tug turned the bow of the *Maria Doria* across the Mississippi River so that the cruise liner faced north.

Once in position, the tug cast off its line and let the liner sail under its own steam. The stern tug kept its line attached in case the *Maria Doria* lost power. Jackson ordered Angelina to proceed. She throttled the engines forward. With a blast of its airhorn, the cruise liner made its way out of port and along the Mississippi.

The trip down river to the ocean covered almost one hundred miles, which meant they would be traveling for several hours. At Algiers Point, the Mississippi veered east and wound its way through the residential neighborhoods of New Orleans. Even at this late hour, the city blazed with lights. Tatyana wondered how long it would be before she returned here, assuming any of them survived the voyage.

Jackson maneuvered the liner through the lazy curves of the river, warning of nearby craft and directing Angelina away from any underwater obstructions. After the Naval Air Station, New Orleans gave way to the smaller towns of the suburbs. Lights still shone in many windows. Tatyana became mesmerized by them, wondering what was happening inside those homes. Couples watching TV together or engaging in more intimate activities. Students up late studying. Parents preparing their kids' meals for school tomorrow. Individuals just getting home from or getting ready to leave for work. People going about their everyday lives.

Something Tatyana would never have.

After thirty miles, the *Maria Doria* sailed along the portion of the Mississippi surrounded on both sides by farmland. No one spoke on the bridge beside the necessary commands for navigating the river. Giselle stayed by herself on the starboard wing while Tatyana and Nick stared out the port side. Even Nick remained silent, a rarity for him.

Soon after, bayous and bays slowly encroached on the farms, with only scattered buildings along both banks. This continued for over an hour until the liner passed Venice, the last town along the Mississippi. Then darkness engulfed everything on either flank of the cruise liner. It appeared as if they were sailing into a void, which made Tatyana uneasy. She stepped to the rear of the bridge and stared behind her. A soft glow emanating from New Orleans a hundred miles away was the only light visible.

At the Head of Passes Light, the Mississippi branched into two smaller estuaries that ran east and southeast while the main river cont southwest. Angelina maneuvered down the latter.

Fletcher stepped over to Tatyana. "We'll reach the Gulf of Mexico in a few minutes. I wanted to let you know so you can be ready if anything happens."

"Thanks."

When the captain had returned to the console, Nick leaned closer. "Are you okay?"

"No," she whispered, staring into the night, trying not to let the uncertainty ahead overwhelm her.

"It can be scary out here. I know."

"You were dealing with *kamikazes* and Japanese submarines. You knew what type of dangers you faced. I have no clue what's going to happen next."

A few minutes later, the *Maria Doria* passed by Pilot Station East, the last location a mile before the Mississippi drained into the Gulf of Mexico.

Jackson stepped away from the console. "We're all clear, captain. The ship is yours."

"Thanks." The two men shook hands. "Mister Daley, please show Mr. Jackson back to his boat."

"Yes, sir." The junior officer stepped forward and motioned to the exit. "If you'll follow me, please."

As the two men left the bridge, Jackson paused and turned to Fletcher. "Good luck. I'm afraid you'll need it."

A few minutes later, Jackson was aboard the pilot boat and heading back to Pilot Station East. The captain waited until he received confirmation that the ship was clear before issuing the next order.

"Miss Rosario, set course bearing 152, speed twenty-two knots."

"Yes, captain," Angelina replied. "Setting course bearing 152, speed twenty-two knots."

The *Maria Doria* increased speed and headed into the Gulf of Mexico, the lights along the Louisiana coast rapidly fading in the distance.

Fletcher moved to the front of the bridge and turned to face his crew. "This is it. We're about to find out for sure whether this liner is haunted. Everyone be on your guard. We'll see what happens next."

CHAPTER ELEVEN

"**W**ELL, THIS IS boring," muttered Nick.

"Tell me about it," whispered Tatyana.

The *Maria Doria* had been at sea for close to three hours, and nothing unusual had happened. The ship functioned perfectly. Fletcher stood near the ECDIS console for the entire voyage, waiting for something to go wrong, though it never did. The captain and crew seemed satisfied with the lack of activity.

The same could not be said of Giselle. She had started the trip brimming with nervous energy, worried that this trip would produce the same negative results. As the hours passed and nothing happened, her nervousness changed to confusion and eventually frustration. She checked her watch for the fifth time in the past hour and huffed.

"How long were you out of port last time when the incident occurred?"

"An hour after we left the Mississippi," replied Fletcher.

"Then what's wrong?"

"Nothing. The ship is performing above standard."

"If the damn ship had done that in the first place, then this wouldn't be an issue," snapped Giselle.

"Do I need to remind you that I'm well aware of what happened on our maiden voyage?" Fletcher's demeanor did not change, though his tone gave Giselle a dressing down. "We lost a good man that afternoon for no reason. I want to find out why just as much as you do, but I'm more interested in the safety of my crew and the passengers than the company's public image."

Angelina smiled. The other two deck officers slightly nodded their heads in appreciation.

The gestures were not lost on Giselle. She turned abruptly toward the bow. Tatyana watched as the belligerence drained out of her. The woman's shoulders slumped, and her body lost its rigidity. After a few seconds, Giselle faced the captain and crew.

"Sorry to be such a bitch. Even though it doesn't sound like it, my priority is ensuring everyone on board is safe." Giselle spoke the words with sincerity.

"Apology accepted," replied the captain.

Giselle motioned for Fletcher to join her. They both approached Tatyana. "Corporate is riding my ass. They called me before we left and implied that if I don't come back with a rational explanation as to what happened, I might as well find another line of work."

"We understand," said Fletcher.

"Tatyana." Giselle chuckled awkwardly. "I'm sure no one has never said this to you before, but please tell me you feel the presence of ghosts on the ship."

Tatyana shook her head. "Sorry, I'm not sensing anything."

"Neither am I," responded Nick.

"That's wonderful," sighed Giselle. "We have no official cause for the incident."

"It might be a freak accident," Nick offered. "They occurred all the time during the war."

"Could it have been a freak accident?" repeated Tatyana.

"It probably was," answered Fletcher. "The problem is, engineers went through every inch of the staff mess and found nothing that could even remotely have caused the fire. It's still an unexplained mystery."

"Without an explanation, it'll be impossible to get the liner to pass inspection." Giselle leaned against the console. Her body sagged. "That means the *Maria Doria* will probably be decommissioned, which is a major loss for the company. Which means corporate will look for a scapegoat to satisfy the shareholders."

"And I assume that's you?" Tatyana already knew the answer to that question.

Giselle scowled and nodded.

Tatyana sympathized with Giselle. The poor woman was only doing her job, yet the higher-ups would throw her and her reputation under the bus without a second thought. Tatyana had faced a similar situation with that asshole Doctor Lasota who nearly derailed her doctorate when she refused to sleep with him. She could not prove the existence of something that refused to reveal itself. However, she could offer Giselle as much cover as possible for the shitstorm the woman would face.

"What time is it?"

Fletcher checked his watch. "A quarter to three."

"Spirits are most active at three in the morning. If you want, I can go down to the crew mess and see if I detect an unnatural presence."

"Are you sure?" asked Giselle.

"I promised to do everything I could to determine if there's paranormal activity on this ship."

"The last time you tried, you didn't have any success." Fletcher didn't seem convinced.

"We were in port. It's possible they're only active at sea."

"Makes sense." The captain nodded and turned to the console. "Miss Rosario, will you escort Miss Reynolds and Miss DeMarco down to the staff mess? I'll take the helm."

"Of course, captain." Angelina stepped away from her post. "Would you ladies follow me, please?"

Nostradamus barked.

"You can join us, boy."

The dog's tail wagged furiously as he followed the three women off the bridge.

✕   ✕   ✕

ANGELINA LED THE way to the staff mess, unlocked the door, and switched on the lights. Once the room was illuminated, she allowed Tatyana, Giselle, and Nostradamus to enter, then followed them inside.

Giselle moved up alongside Tatyana, her eyes pleading. "I know you're doing this to cover my ass, and I appreciate it. If you detect anything, even the slightest presence of a ghost, please report it."

"You know I will."

As the other two women positioned themselves by the exit, Tatyana moved into the center of the mess hall.

Nick exited the kitchen. "There's nothing here."

"What about that slight hum we picked up last time?"

"I feel that, but it's background noise, more than likely left over from when the staff captain died."

"What did you say?" Giselle asked from across the mess hall.

"I'm just summoning the spirits," lied Tatyana.

Even though she figured it would be futile, Tatyana closed her eyes and opened her senses, welcoming the spirits to contact her. Like the first time, she was unable to detect any paranormal activity.

"Are you picking up anything?" asked Nick.

Tatyana did not. She glanced down at Nostradamus, who had laid down and spread himself on the floor.

Tatyana wandered around the staff mess for ten minutes, occasionally pausing to open herself to any spectral presence, but not sensing anything. She made her way into the kitchen, following the same procedure and coming up with the same results.

"There's nothing here," said Nick, who followed her.

"I know. I'm going to attempt to summon them again."

"Okay, but it's a waste of time."

Tatyana knew he was right but wanted to try for Giselle's sake. She left the kitchen and stood in the center of the mess hall.

"I'm calling on the spirit or spirits who reside on this ship. I want to talk with you."

As expected, there was no change in the spectral aura.

"To the spirit or spirits who reside here, please contact me. I mean you no harm. I only wish to talk."

Still nothing.

"If there are any spirits here, I demand you contact me. Show yourselves and make your presence known."

Still no change in the spectral aura.

"Anything?" asked Giselle.

"Nope. Sorry."

"Shit," mumbled Giselle.

Tatyana came over, placed an arm around the woman's shoulder, and hugged her.

"Let's head back to the bridge," suggested Angelina. "We need to inform the captain that we didn't find anything."

✕　✕　✕

ONCE BACK ON the bridge, Tatyana briefed Captain Fletcher on what they found or, more appropriately, didn't find. He said nothing until she finished, then asked, "So you're saying there are no ghosts, spirits, or paranormal activity aboard the *Maria Doria?*"

"Yes."

"And that conclusion will be included in your final assessment to the board of directors?"

"Yes."

"Miss DeMarco, do you concur with Miss Reynolds' findings?"

Giselle hesitated, knowing her answer would not be well

received by corporate. Finally, she replied, "I do."

"Then I plan on returning to New Orleans." Fletcher offered Giselle one final way to save face. "Do you concur?"

Giselle closed her eyes and nodded.

Fletcher turned to the officers manning the bridge. "Miss Rosario, set a course that will return us to New Orleans and then radio ahead that we'll need a pilot to guide us in."

"Yes, captain. Setting course back to New Orleans."

Angelina checked the radar. The only other vessel within the area was a large ship approaching from the south one mile to port, allowing them plenty of room to maneuver. She turned to the comms officer.

"Miss Hashimoto, please contact the approaching vessel via VHF and confirm that we'll be conducting a port to starboard passing."

"Yes, ma'am."

"Helm, maintain heading. Keep a mile distance between us."

"Maintaining heading," responded Campbell.

With the other ship notified of their intention, Angelina moved the controls to steer the *Maria Doria* starboard.

Nothing happened. The liner remained on its current course.

She attempted the maneuver a second time with the same lack of results.

"Captain Fletcher, we have a problem."

"What is it?"

Angelina met his gaze, a tinge of fear in her eyes. "We've lost navigational control of the ship."

CHAPTER TWELVE

ALTHOUGH HE MAINTAINED his professionalism, a look of concern washed across Fletcher's face. "Are you certain about that?"

"Yes, sir."

Giselle looked out over the bow of the cruise liner. "Then why are we turning?"

"I'm not doing that, ma'am. The ship has set its own course fifteen degrees to starboard. The same heading as before." She tried to turn the wheel and resume course, but it would not budge. Angelina looked up at Fletcher. "The rudder won't respond."

"Which is exactly what happened on our first voyage." Fletcher moved in front of Campbell. "What type of ship is to our port?"

Campbell checked the radar. "It's the *Amyntas*, a ULCC tanker."

"Captain," began Angelina. "We were passing a tanker last time when the ship refused to respond and changed course on its own."

The crew focused on the fire indicator light, expecting it to glow. It did not. Fletcher toggled the security cameras until he located the one in the staff mess. Nothing went on in the area.

Giselle raced over to Tatyana. "Do you sense anything?"

"Let me check." Tatyana closed her eyes and cleared her mind of all thoughts, concentrating on any spectral presence. The dull background hum she detected earlier remained, only now slightly more intense.

"I don't feel any significant change in the ship's aura," offered Nick, who stood a few feet behind her.

Tatyana opened her eyes. "I'm not getting anything."

The captain joined them. "If it was a ghost taking control of the ship, would you detect it?"

"I should be able to."

"That settles it," said Fletcher. "We're looking at an internal malfunction."

Tatyana forced a smile. "Sorry."

"No need to apologize, ma'am. You just confirmed that the problem is mechanical, not spiritual."

"Should I stop the ship?" asked Angelina.

"Not yet. Decrease speed to twelve knots. And send out a message that we've lost control of the vessel."

"Decreasing speed to twelve knots."

Fletcher picked up the phone and dialed the engine room. "Engineering, this is the captain. We've lost control of the ship again."

"Damn it," replied Sprague. "I was hoping the other time had been a fluke."

"It doesn't look like it. What's your status?"

Fletcher heard Sprague cover the phone with his hand and yell something to one of the other crew members. A moment later, the chief of engineering came back on.

"Like last time, we have no indications anything is wrong with the rudder. Do you want me to try and set course manually?"

"Please. Reset course to bearing 152."

Fletcher waited a few minutes for Sprague to come back on. "Not surprising, the rudder isn't responding. I'll have my men check on it."

"Keep me posted." Fletcher hung up the phone and turned to Angelina. "We'll maintain a speed of twelve knots until we either fix the rudder or—"

Nostradamus jumped up from the deck and whined. His

ears folded back against his head and his tail wrapped underneath his body. Suddenly, the dog moved closer to Tatyana and howled.

As he did, the fire indicator light glowed red.

"Captain," said Angelina. "We have indications of a fire."

"Let me guess. The staff mess."

"Yes, sir."

Fletcher stepped over to the console and checked the video feed of the staff mess. No fire was visible.

From behind Tatyana, Nick moaned. "Be careful. There's a huge spike in the—"

Before he could finish his sentence, the surge in the spectral aura hit Tatyana, overwhelming her senses. She fell back against the bulkhead. Anguish. Terror. Hatred. Revenge. The emotions filled her soul and clouded her mind. Emotions not from one entity but many. Too many for her to count. She pressed her fingers against her temple, trying to regain her composure.

Giselle ran over and placed a hand on Tatyana's shoulder. "Are you okay?"

Tatyana waved her off, concentrating instead on refocusing her attention.

Nick came over and crouched beside her. "Concentrate on your thoughts."

"I can't. They won't let go."

"Who won't let go?" asked Giselle.

Fletcher motioned for the woman not to talk.

"Focus on my voice," urged Nick. "Ignore them. They sense you. They know you can hear their cries."

"I'm not up to this." Tatyana felt as though she was going insane.

"Yes, you are. You defeated Kathleen and Eliza. You can push these out of your mind."

"There are too many!"

"Concentrate on me."

"I can't."

"You have to," demanded Nick. "You can't let them gain control over you."

Numerous voices talked to her at once from the supernatural world. Tatyana tried to block them out, but there were too many. She could barely discern Nick among the cacophony. Focus on Nick, Tatyana told herself to no avail. Negativity flooded her mind, drowning out Nick, drowning out her thoughts. She had never felt so powerless against the spirits. It seemed as if they wanted to drag her down.

The focus she needed came not from Nick's voice but from a warm wetness engulfing her face. Tatyana opened her eyes. Nostradamus stood beside her, licking her. Tatyana's mind shifted from the vengeful souls tearing at her mind and soul to the unconditional love of her pet, bringing her back to reality.

The grip of the spirit world gave way, allowing Tatyana to reassert dominance. She clasped Nostradamus' cheeks in her hand and rubbed her nose against his. Only then did she notice that her hands shook and sweat engulfed her body. She inhaled deeply and held it for ten seconds to calm herself. Releasing the breath, Tatyana moved her hands up and scratched behind the dog's ears.

"Who's a good boy?"

The wagging of his tail indicated they both knew the answer to that question.

"Are you okay?" asked Fletcher.

"I am now. They caught me off guard."

Giselle arched her eyebrows. "*They?*"

Tatyana nodded. "There's more than one aboard this ship."

"How many?" The question came from the captain.

"Dozens. And they possess the most malevolent aura I've ever felt."

"That's not good." Fletcher considered his options. "What's the next step?"

"I head down to the staff mess and see if I can communicate with them."

"No. It's too dangerous."

"The only way I can cleanse them from the *Maria Doria* is to find out who they are and why they're possessing the ship."

"There has to be another option."

"You could scuttle it." Tatyana said it as a joke.

Giselle took it seriously. "I can't suggest that. Corporate would fire me on the spot."

"I don't give a shit what corporate thinks," responded Fletcher in an uncommon burst of anger that startled Giselle. "My responsibility is to the safety of the passengers and crew, not making sure the shareholders get a profit."

Giselle lowered her head.

Fletcher turned to Tatyana. "That responsibility includes making sure you're safe, Miss Reynolds."

"I appreciate your concern. But my job is to remove lingering spirits and send them to their afterlife. It's as much for their benefit as for the living."

"Understood." Fletcher nodded his understanding. "However, you're not going alone. Miss DeMarco and Miss Rosario will accompany you. Bring a radio so you can keep in touch with the bridge. And if there is any indication that an incident might happen like the one that killed Staff Captain Sullivan, even if it's only a gut feeling, the three of you get out of there and return to the bridge." He made eye contact with Angelina. "That's an order."

"Yes, sir." Angelina grabbed a radio from its mount as Tatyana slung the travel bag of ingredients over her shoulder. The officer escorted Tatyana, Giselle, and Nostradamus off the bridge.

Nick followed, wanting to stay close in case anything happened.

✕   ✕   ✕

A FEW MINUTES later, they reached deck two and entered the main corridor heading toward the staff mess. The closer they got, the more intense the spectral auras became. This time, Tatyana anticipated the onslaught of emotions and was able to deal with the sensations. They were much stronger down here than on the bridge. And more numerous. She detected scores of different auras but could not determine precisely how many. All of them endured anguish and terror. Nearly half were consumed by hatred. The sense of malevolence emanating from the staff mess overpowered everything else.

Tatyana reached for the doorknob, but Angelina stopped her. "Let me check in with the bridge." She keyed the talk button. "We're at the staff mess now and are about to enter."

"We have you on the security camera," responded Fletcher. "So far, there are no changes. The fire indicator is still on for that area, but the cameras show no activity. If you still plan on going ahead with this, proceed with extreme caution."

"Don't worry. If anything happens out of the ordinary, we'll haul ass out of here faster than you've ever seen."

A chuckle came across the radio, and the captain closed with, "Good luck."

Angelina placed the top of her left hand on the metal door, feeling for any signs of an inferno on the other side. It was cool to the touch. She gestured for the other women and the dog to stand to one side. When they did, Angelina opened the door a few inches, bracing herself for flames to shoot out.

Nothing happened.

All three women sighed with relief. Nostradamus looked between the three humans, confused.

Angelina met Tatyana's gaze. "Are you ready?"

"Ready as I'll ever be."

"Any sign of trouble, we bug out. I'm not taking any

chances, not after what happened to Brendan. Clear?"

Tatyana and Giselle responded, "Clear."

Angelina nodded and led the way into the staff mess.

CHAPTER THIRTEEN

T HE PRESENCE OF spirits swarmed around Tatyana the moment she stepped across the threshold. She closed her mind to them individually, focusing instead on the situation.

Angelina started to close the door, but Tatyana stopped her. "Keep it open. I don't know how this is going to pan out. If it goes south, head for safety and don't wait for me."

Neither woman had to be told twice.

Nick moved up alongside Tatyana. "We caught them off guard."

"You mean they're afraid of us?"

"No, just wary. They sense we can communicate with them on their level."

"Who are you talking to?" asked Giselle.

Tatyana ignored her and moved to where the staff captain had been incinerated. "Do you know how many there are?"

"Too many to count. I suggest we start the cleansing before they figure out who we are and why we're here."

"Agreed. Cover me while I prepare."

Tatyana placed the travel bag on the floor, opened it, and removed a container of kosher salt and nine Selenite crystals, one of which she slipped into her pocket. She stepped over to the women.

"What's going on?" Giselle insisted. "And who are you talking to?"

"I don't have time to explain. Stand still and do exactly as I tell you." Tatyana handed each of them three Selenite crystals. "Put one of these in each of your pockets. Don't lose them no matter what. Understand?"

They nodded.

Tatyana snapped her fingers and motioned for Nostrada-mus to stand between the two women. The dog obeyed. She opened the spout on the container and created a protective circle around them, then stood back several feet. Tatyana recited the warfare prayer used in cleansing stubborn entities.

"I address myself to the purest entities of the spiritual world. I ask you to grant me the power to overcome fear and darkness. Forgive my sins and imperfections, cleanse my soul, and imbue me with the courage to confront and defeat the vile entities before me. By all that is good and holy, I bow in humility before you and ask that you cover me with the white light and protection of the purest spirits. I claim the protection of this light for myself, for my friends, and for all those aboard this ship. I take a stand against all that is evil and negative. In the name of the purest entities of the spiritual world, I com-mand the entities that have taken a life in this room to reveal themselves."

"I'd move this along," urged Nick. "Whatever is down here is getting agitated."

"Have they tried speaking to you?"

"No. But they're pissed off big time."

Tatyana removed another container of salt and created a circle around herself.

Nick moved up beside her. "Don't waste time with the incantation. I think they're getting ready to strike."

Tatyana closed her mind and focused on the ship's spectral aura. Anger, hatred, and vengeance seethed through the staff mess. She sensed they were all in danger.

"I give myself to the purest entities of the spiritual world. I refuse to show fear and back down from the darkness that haunts this cruise ship."

The aura wavered momentarily.

"I'm here to help."

Scores of voices spoke to Tatyana simultaneously, male and female, each with a different accent and each filled with rage.

"*Help us? How?*"

"I'm here to help you move on to your afterlife."

"*What do we care about that? Our lives were stolen from us. We were of no value to them. They let us suffer and die.*"

"Who are 'they'?"

The voices remained quiet.

"How did you die?"

"*In agony.*"

"I'm sorry. There is nothing I can do to ease your suffering. But I can help you move on to a better place."

"*A better place?*" The collective laugh of so many tormented souls made Tatyana's blood run cold. "*There is no such thing for us. We died because of arrogance and incompetence. We are bound to this realm because of greed. Only one thing can free us from this plain of existence.*"

"What's that?" Tatyana wasn't sure if she wanted to hear the answer.

The voices spoke in unison. Half uttered the word *justice*. The other half said *revenge*.

"That's not true," Giselle yelled from inside her salt circle.

Tatyana felt the aura shift its attention from her to Giselle. The aura moved away from Tatyana and hovered in front of Giselle for a few seconds before materializing into a corporeal form.

The lone figure floated in front of Giselle, translucent and shimmering. Its form changed several times a second, as if someone had a slide projector and rapidly advanced the images. Each alteration displayed a figure of a different sex, ethnicity, height, and size. The only consistency was that they all wore white cruise line uniforms and had expressions of loathing and rage on their faces. Its eyes widened in recognition and squinted in hatred. The voice grew dark and angry.

"*You are one of them!*"

Giselle ignored the allegation. "No one intended to disrespect you."

"*You lie! You desecrated the ground on which we died and showed no respect for us.*"

"That wasn't me." Giselle's plea nearly devolved into tears.

"*You may not have made the decisions, but you are one of them.*"

"Please forgive us."

"*Forgiveness? Not for your willful desecration. The only thing that will satisfy us is….*" Here the voices separated, once again half speaking *justice* and the other half *revenge*.

"Wait," called out Tatyana. The spectral image turned to face her. "I'm the one who can help you, but I have no idea what you're talking about. How did you die? How were you desecrated?"

The spirit pointed to Giselle. "*She can tell you about how our souls were deemed meaningless, not that any of this is your concern. But if you persist in knowing how we died, we'll let you experience those moments.*"

Before Tatyana could protest, the entity engulfed her. Tatyana's consciousness left her body and became immersed in the world of the tormented souls.

Tatyana stood on the bridge of another cruise liner. It was daytime. Dense fog shrouded the vessel. She recognized the crew from among the changing faces within the spirit. Only now, panic and urgency had set in. The ship's horn blared continuously. The helmsman swung the ship hard to port. The captain braced himself against the ECDIS console, one hand on the edge and the other clutching a microphone. He yelled into it, though the only word Tatyana could make out above all the noise was "brace." An officer stood on the bridge wing, repeatedly firing a flare gun into the sky. Every member of the crew kept staring to their right. Tatyana did the same and immediately wished she hadn't.

Tatyana gasped as an oil tanker nearly two hundred feet long bore down on them, rapidly emerging from the fog.

The tanker must have spotted them at the last minute because it veered hard to starboard. Like those on the bridge, she knew the tanker had not initiated the turn in time. A collision was inevitable. Due to the tanker's speed and size, if it rammed the cruise liner at a right angle, the tanker would have gouged a massive hole into the liner's starboard side and likely sink it.

Instead, the tanker hit at a fifty-degree angle, its bow colliding into the liner's mid-section behind the bridge. Both vessels ground against each other for several seconds. The upper decks of the cruise liner buckled, gouging their way through the port hull of the tanker for almost one hundred feet. Gasoline poured out of the rupture, dousing the starboard side of the cruise liner. Due to the liner tilting to port as the two ships collided, the gasoline ran across the decks to the other side. A large pool flowed into the bridge.

The two vessels eventually moved away from each other. At the last second, a stray chunk of steel gashed out of the tanker's port side scraped along the liner's Lido deck guardrail, generating a spark. Within seconds, the top decks of the cruise liner became a sea of flames. It flowed along the deck, igniting the gasoline in the bridge. The crew died within seconds, including many of the senior officers. For a moment, Tatyana felt the fire as it scorched her skin and melted her muscles. Experienced the agony as the blood boiled in her veins. Breathed in the flames that instantly seared out her lungs. She clutched at her chest, desperate to take in air.

Tatyana suddenly appeared in the radio room, watching as the officer on duty attempted to contact someone... anyone... who could send help. She experienced his panic and frustration, her heart pounding in her chest and her inhaling difficult because of the heat and smoke. The flames had destroyed all means of communication. The officer even tried using his cellphone, but no satellite connection could be made this far out at sea. He continued until the conflagration made it impossible to remain at his station. Overcome by defeat, the officer left his post and headed for the bow.

Tatyana jumped from one part of the burning cruise liner to another, witnessing the nightmare from the perspective of various crew members, and experiencing the emotions and physical pain they endured. She found herself as part of a firefighting team hosing down the flames on B deck when gasoline poured through the air ducts and ignited when it came in contact with the flames, instantly incinerating the crew. Then as one of the engineers forced to cut power to the engines so the ship wouldn't become a hazard to others before seeking an escape from the lowest parts of the ship, only to suffocate in a passageway when the oxygen was sucked out to feed the raging inferno. Other crew members tried to make their way topside, only to find every path blocked by flames, forcing them deeper into the ship. Every spirit forced her to experience their ordeal at once, the nightmares of more than a hundred souls condensed into a few minutes.

One by one, those crewmen who did not die in the initial blaze were herded by the flames into a single room near the bow of the cruise liner. It appeared strikingly similar to the staff mess aboard the *Maria Doria*. Nearly seventy-five men and women crowded into this confined space as the inferno drew nearer. Being below the waterline, no portholes were available to offer even a modicum of escape. Panic overwhelmed the crew. Some prayed. Many broke down and cried. One young woman ran into the kitchen, removed a carving knife from the drawer, and deeply sliced the blade along both arms, from the inner elbows to the wrists, preferring to die peacefully. Many pushed their way into the kitchen and the far corner of the hall to get as far away from the flames as possible. Even the few who maintained their calm were terrified.

Smoke flowed under the doors. Several crew members took off their shirts and jackets, stuffing them into the open spaces. Many burned their hands on the steel doors, which absorbed the heat from the conflagration making its way down the corridor. No sooner had they stemmed the flow when smoke poured from the air ducts and drifted to the ceiling, rapidly filling the staff mess.

Tatyana was among the trapped personnel, experiencing the same emotions as the spirits did in those last moments of their lives. The overwhelming terror. The desperation to survive mixed with the frustrating realization that they would not. The regrets and anger. The mental breakdowns and surges of faith. Everyone's tormented final moments.

The temperature climbed inside the staff mess until it reached over one hundred and thirty degrees. Quite a few passed out from the heat. Those still conscious found breathing difficult, a factor compounded by the heavy black smoke pouring in from the air ducts. In the corridor, the roar drew closer until it reached the staff mess. Within seconds, the steel door steamed. The clothing stuffed in the open space burst into flames. Embers floated through the air, landing on and igniting the flammable surfaces near the doors. The last few crew members with an ounce of rationality grabbed fire extinguishers off the walls and tried to put it out, a futile gesture that bought them seconds at most. Once inside the room, the fire spread quickly. Crew members vainly battling the flames were unfortunate enough to have their clothes ignite, suffering the torment of being burned alive. The fortunate ones suffocated as the fire sucked all the oxygen out of the confined space, leaving lifeless bodies to be later consumed by the flames.

Tatyana glanced around as the staff mess became one massive inferno, burning like the inside of a furnace. Flames engulfed her. In addition to experiencing the combined emotions of those about to die, Tatyana also suffered the anguish of each person's death—the suffocations, the searing of flesh and muscles, the boiling of blood in their veins. Any one of these death throes would be agonizing enough. To endure the torment of more than seventy people dying at once was maddening.

Tatyana struggled to maintain a grip on her sanity, telling herself none of this was real, that she merely experienced the nightmare they had gone through. Still, the suffering she endured, even if on an existential level, proved beyond comprehension. She fell to her knees, closing her eyes and placing her hands over her ears to block out the surrounding sensations. Tatyana concentrated on reality, not the spectral realm she had been dragged into. She told herself it would be over in a minute. She needed to focus on her physical location. Yet the torments, though imaginary, were too much. She felt as though she would soon join them aboard—

Something touched Tatyana on the face. She screamed, yanking herself back to reality. She still knelt within the salt circle, only now her body trembled. Sweat drenched her clothes. Nostradamus stood in front of her, his face inches from her own. Nick hovered directly behind the dog, a concerned expression on his face.

"Are you okay?"

"I'll be fine." Tatyana leaned on Nostradamus for support. "But this is much worse than we ever imagined."

"How so?"

"More than a hundred people died aboard this ship in the most horrifying way imaginable."

"*You now understand what we endured,*" said the spirit's voice from behind Tatyana.

She jumped up and spun around to face the ghastly apparition, gasping at the image that confronted her. The corporeal visage still changed constantly, taking the form of one victim before quickly morphing into another. Only now, each tormented soul appeared as a charred corpse.

"I had no idea."

"*It does not matter. You are irrelevant to us. The one we want is....*" It floated across the staff mess and stopped in front of Giselle. Its right arm raised, pointing an accusatory finger at the terrified woman.

"*Her.*"

"Why me?"

The voices of over one hundred souls cried out simultaneously. "*We seek atonement.*"

"I didn't do anything." Giselle looked at Tatyana and Angelina. "I swear."

"*You represent those who did. You knew the situation and said nothing, endangering the lives of everyone aboard this ship. Your callousness cannot go unpunished.*"

"What do you want from me?" Giselle verged on the brink of tears.

Its voice grew dark and malevolent. "*Your soul.*"

"No." Giselle fell back, stepping outside the salt circle.

"Stay inside where you'll be safe," warned Tatyana.

"*Stay out of this!*" The entity spun around to face her, its translucent image fluctuating in fury.

"I'm not going to let you kill an innocent person."

"*She is far from innocent. If you persist in interfering, we have no qualms in taking your soul as well.*"

Tatyana tapped down her fear, replacing it with defiance. "Good luck with that."

The spirit elevated several feet above the deck and spread its arms wide. A glow emanated from it, starting out white and changing color to a fiery hue. Then a spark of fire formed above its head, flowing along either side until it formed a circle of flames around the entity. Once completed, the circle grew in intensity. At least now Tatyana knew how Brendan had died. She braced herself for her demise.

Nick positioned himself in front of Tatyana. "I won't let you do this."

The spirit said nothing. It merely leveled its left hand toward Nick and flicked its fingers. A small ball of fire no larger than a grapefruit flew out of its palm, engulfing Nick and carrying him away. Both disappeared through the hull.

On seeing the fireball, Giselle panicked and ran for the

open door. It shut suddenly, trapping the woman inside. The spirit spun around to face her, the ring of flames still encircling it.

"We will now have justice / revenge."

Giselle leaned against the door, turned her head to one side, and closed her eyes tight, prepared for her demise.

With the entity distracted, Tatyana crouched, withdrew a container of kosher salt from her travel bag, and twisted off the cardboard top. She rushed toward the entity, shoving her hand forward and simultaneously spinning it. The entire contents of the container covered its back.

"In the name of the purest entities of the spiritual world, I command you leave at once. I ban you from ever returning."

The circle of flame died out. Its corporeal form waivered. The spirit spun around, fury in its eyes, its gaze locked on Tatyana. It uttered a single warning as it broke apart and drifted away. Not a shout or a cry of anger. To Tatyana, that would have been preferable. Instead, the hundred or so voices spoke in unison, quietly but with dark intent.

"You will suffer for this."

The entity collapsed in on itself and disappeared in a puff. Only a lingering hint of its malevolence remained.

Tatyana did not want to wait around and see if it returned. She ran back, grabbed her bag, and headed for the exit. Nostradamus followed, protecting his mistress. Angelina had already tried the door. Thankfully, it was unlocked. She ushered the shaken Giselle into the corridor. When Tatyana joined them, they made their way to the bridge.

CHAPTER FOURTEEN

W HEN THE GROUP returned to the bridge, Fletcher excused himself and led the ladies to a small stateroom down the corridor. Nostradamus and Nick followed. Once inside, the captain gestured for Tatyana and Giselle to take the seats in front of his desk, which they did. Nostradamus curled up beside his mistress. Angelina stood behind them. Nick leaned against the wall beside the door.

Fletcher opened his lower desk drawer, removed a bottle of Maker's Mark whiskey and three tumblers, and filled each halfway. He offered one to Tatyana and Giselle. Tatyana declined. Giselle grabbed her tumbler and gulped down the contents in one long swig, then took the one offered to her friend. Fletcher picked the third tumbler off his desk and handed it to Angelina.

She waved it away. "I can't. I'm still on duty."

"After what you just went through, I can excuse it this time."

"Thanks, but I prefer to keep my senses."

Fletcher nodded his approval and slid into the leather chair behind his desk. "All right. Tell me everything that happened down in the staff mess."

Tatyana spent the next forty-five minutes providing precise details of the occurrence from the moment they had entered the staff mess until their hasty retreat, especially the visions she received from the spirits. Angelina occasionally chimed in to verify some of the more bizarre aspects of Tatyana's story. Giselle said nothing. She finished the second tumbler in one gulp and nursed along the one Angelina had refused. When Tatyana finished, they all focused on Fletcher, waiting for his response.

The captain leaned back in his chair and studied them for a few seconds, his expression stoic. At first, Tatyana worried he did not believe them. Not that she could blame him. She would not believe the story if she had not been doing this type of work for the past year. Tatyana started to plan out how she would respond to the captain's dismissal when Fletcher sat forward and rested his arms on the desk.

"Everything you said confirms what we saw on the security camera."

"Even the ring of fire?" asked Tatyana.

"Yes. And I have to admit, that freaked the shit out of me."

"I have a question." Angelina moved alongside Tatyana's chair. "Who were you talking to in the staff mess?"

Fletcher seemed confused. "I thought it was to you or Miss DeMarco."

Angelina shook her head.

From behind her, Nick said, "You might as well tell them."

"Are you sure?" questioned Tatyana.

"In for a penny."

Fletcher glanced around the room. "Who are you talking to?"

"Nick. He's a spirit I met on my first paranormal investigation. He's been helping me ever since."

"Are you two...." Angelina struggled to put it in polite terms.

"Romantic?"

"She wishes," quipped Nick.

Tatyana glared at him out of the corner of her eye. "Nick has insights into the paranormal realm that have proven useful. Nothing more. He's here with us now."

"Can he make his presence known?"

"How?"

Angelina thought for a moment. "I don't know. Can he knock one of the tumblers off the desk?"

Nick snorted. "I'm not a cat."

Tatyana suppressed a grin. "How about something more involved?"

"Make him turn the lights on and off," suggested Fletcher.

"That's more like it." Nick went over to the switch and flipped it on and off nine times, three times quickly, three slowly, and the last three quickly.

Fletcher caught the reference and nodded. "Thank you for helping us, Nick."

"I have a question." Tatyana shifted in her chair to face Giselle. "Why were the entities so angry at you?"

Giselle finished off the third tumbler in one large swig. "I don't know what you mean."

Tatyana did not back down. "They blamed their situation on you, saying you represented those who caused their torment and accused you of endangering everyone's life. They wanted to take their revenge on you. Why do they think that?"

Giselle moved forward in her chair and reached for the bottle of whiskey.

Fletcher pulled it toward him. "Tell us what you know."

Giselle leaned back. "The ghosts technically don't belong aboard the *Maria Doria*. They died on the *Caribbean Dream*."

Angelina looked between Giselle and the captain. "Why does that name sound familiar?"

"The *Caribbean Dream* belonged to Miami Cruise Lines. It was decommissioned twenty months ago due to structural issues."

Giselle averted her gaze.

Fletcher became angry but kept his emotions in check. "I think it's time you fess up, Miss DeMarco."

Giselle refused to talk.

"You have to tell us everything," urged Tatyana. "The spirits below deck are pissed at us, and everyone aboard this ship is in danger. We need to know why."

"The structural issues that put the *Caribbean Dream* out of commission were the result of a massive fire that destroyed over seventy-five percent of the ship." Giselle raised her head. "The *Caribbean Dream* was making a run to New Orleans. The passengers and hotel staff had left the ship in Miami, and the deck crew were bringing the ship here to pick up new hotel staff and passengers. There were one hundred and thirteen personnel on board. They were sailing through a heavy fog about twenty miles south of Key West when the *Ise Maru*, a Japanese oil tanker, ran into the ship. One of the fuel container tanks ruptured and covered the *Caribbean Dream* in gasoline, which ignited. The flames took out the bridge within minutes and knocked out communications. Those not killed trying to save the ship were forced to seek shelter in the staff mess where the fire eventually burned them alive."

"Why didn't the Coast Guard help them?" asked Fletcher.

Giselle sighed. "After the accident, it was one screw-up after another. The bridge crew on the *Ise Maru* were incompetent and never told the Coast Guard they had rammed a cruise liner, probably trying to hide their mistake. By the time the Coast Guard arrived, the *Caribbean Dream* had drifted so far from the scene of the accident that no one could see them due to the fog. It was a good eighteen hours before the weather cleared and an observation plane spotted the liner. By then, the fire had burned itself out and everyone on board was dead."

"Why didn't we ever hear about this?" asked Angelina.

"Because neither side wanted to make the facts public. The company that owned the *Ise Maru* knew they would be hit with so many lawsuits that they'd probably go out of business. And corporate was afraid that if news got out about what happened to the *Caribbean Dream*, tourists might not book cruises because our safety record had been tarnished."

Angelina sneered. "So, everything was brushed under the table."

Giselle nodded. "Since no tourists were involved, the company that owned the tanker paid major compensations to the victims' families as long as they signed NDAs and reimbursed Miami Cruise Lines for the cost of the *Caribbean Dream*."

Tatyana turned to Fletcher. "Did you know any of this?"

"I knew the *Caribbean Dream* had been taken out of service and decommissioned, but this is the first time I've heard the details." The captain focused his attention back on Giselle. "I don't understand why the ghosts are haunting this ship."

Giselle grew agitated, wringing her hands and tapping her left foot on the carpet. She averted her gaze again. "The *Maria Doria* was under construction at the time. It's the sister ship of the *Caribbean Dream*. Before sending the *Caribbean Dream* off to Turkey to be taken apart, corporate stripped it off everything salvageable that could be used in the *Maria Doria*. That included the kitchen appliances in the staff mess."

"Son of a bitch," muttered Nick.

Tatyana agreed with the sentiment. "You're telling me that to cut corners and save a few dollars, the cruise line removed the cooking appliances from the room in which so many crew members were burned alive and installed them on this ship?"

Giselle nodded without raising her head.

"And you never thought to warn me about this when you hired me?" snapped Tatyana.

"That's unfair." Giselle looked into Tatyana's eyes, her own brimming with guilt. "To be perfectly honest, I never put stock in Brendan's death being related to anything supernatural. I always assumed it was the result of some freak accident we'd never find the cause of."

"Still, you didn't think to warn me of any of this when you hired me?"

"I... I assumed all this paranormal stuff was bullshit."

"Do you still think it's bullshit?" asked Angelina.

"Not anymore." Giselle returned her attention to Tatyana. "One of the bigwigs in the main office wanted to cover all the angles. I was told to find someone with a good reputation to conduct the investigation, which is why I picked you."

"I'm honored."

"Honestly," pleaded Giselle. "If I thought there was even the slightest possibility of this being related to a haunting, I would have fully disclosed it to you ahead of time."

An awkward silence fell across the cabin. Tatyana was not sure whether she believed Giselle. She felt confident none of the others did.

Fletcher spoke first. "Miss DeMarco, I'll deal with you and corporate later. Right now, we have to resolve the issue of the ghosts aboard the ship. Miss Reynolds, can you get rid of them?"

"I'm not sure."

Giselle raised her head. "You told me you've done this before."

"I have, but only with single spirits. There was only one evil entity at Eden Hollow and in Salem. And I had a difficult time cleansing them. Now we're dealing with more than a hundred. All of whom will be coming at me at once."

"Does that mean it's impossible?" asked Angelina.

Tatyana thought carefully about her answer. "It might be."

Fletcher nodded his head in understanding. "What can we do to even the odds?"

"You said they never materialized while in port, correct?"

The others responded in the affirmative.

"It's obvious we can't take them on out here where they're the most powerful. I suggest we head back to New Orleans and do the cleansing there."

"In port?" Giselle sounded incredulous. "Where everyone in the city could watch? That would be a PR nightmare for the company."

"Screw the public relations aspect," said Fletcher. "Corporate deserves what it gets. But wouldn't that put the lives of those nearby in danger?"

"He has a point," added Nick.

"It might." Tatyana considered the possibilities. "I can't guarantee that they won't lash out at the innocent."

"Does it have to be in port?" suggested Angelina. "There are huge portions of Louisiana on either side of the Mississippi that are nothing but bayou. We could anchor off any of them and perform the ritual. Whatever happens, it won't pose a threat to the public, and we'd still be close to shore in case we had to abandon ship."

"I like that idea," said Fletcher. Then, to Tatyana, "Do you think that'll work?"

"It's the safest bet," she replied. "We could even evacuate the crew during the ritual and have them return when we're done."

Fletcher seemed satisfied. "Then it's settled. We'll—"

Angelina's radio squawked, interrupting the captain. "Bridge to Angelina. Is the captain with you?"

Angelina removed the radio from her belt and pressed the talk button. "He's here and listening."

"We need him up here. It's urgent."

"We'll be right there."

They rushed out of the stateroom and headed for the bridge. Pandemonium greeted them.

"What's going on?" asked Fletcher.

Campbell teetered on the verge of panic. "The ship is on bearing 123, and its speed is at full throttle."

"Why did you do that?"

"The ship did. It's heading into the middle of the Gulf."

"Shut down the engines."

"We tried but without success." Campbell stared at the captain. "We have no control over the ship."

"The spirits know what we're planning and are trying to prevent it." Tatyana said it to no one in particular.

"That's not the worst of it." Campbell swallowed hard. "We're heading directly for a Category 4 hurricane bearing down on the Gulf."

CHAPTER FIFTEEN

I
F FLETCHER WAS rattled, he did not show it. "Are there any other vessels nearby?"

"Not at the moment."

"Thank God for that. What did the Coast Guard say when you notified them?"

"We haven't been able to. We've lost all communications except those within the ship."

"Damn it." Fletcher changed the topic without hesitating. "I assume you've already informed the chief engineer?"

"Yes, sir. I did before calling you."

"Excellent. Confirm our current position and estimate our course."

"Yes, captain."

Fletcher picked up the phone and called engineering. Sprague answered on the eighth ring, annoyed.

"I'm working on the problem, but I can't fix it if you keep bothering me."

"This is Captain Fletcher."

The voice on the other end suddenly became apologetic. "Sorry, captain. I had no—"

"Understandable. Update me on the situation."

"The ship has changed course to heading 123 and increased speed to full throttle. The rudder is locked."

"What about the second steering motor?"

"They're both on, but the rudder won't budge. I've sent down a crew to move it manually. As for the engines, we can't regain control of the speed."

"Can you shut them down?"

"We've been trying, but without success."

"What about cutting off the fuel supply?"

"Way ahead of you on that. That failed as well. It's like something has control over the ship and refuses to let us in." A tense pause. "Just like last time."

"Do whatever you can to regain control. We can't let the ship operate on its own."

"Roger that."

Fletcher replaced the receiver and turned to Tatyana. "Based on our previous experience, the ghosts won't give us back control of the ship until they've taken a life, and that's a trade I'm not willing to make. Assuming the only way we can regain control is to get rid of these things, are you up to it considering how many ghosts there are?"

Tatyana's body went tense. "I guess I have to be."

From the other end of the bridge, Nick warned, "You're in way over your head on this one."

"I don't have much choice, do I?"

Fletcher moved up alongside Tatyana. "Talking with your ghost friend?"

"Yes."

"If you did this in front of me yesterday, I would have pegged you as nuts. What's he saying?"

"Nick thinks cleansing so many entities will be tough."

"Tough?" Nick blurted. "Given their number and the fact they all want to kill you, it'll be damn near impossible."

"Do you think you can do it?" asked Fletcher.

"I'll try. Worst case scenario, I fail, they take my soul, then give you back control of the ship."

"Unacceptable. I'm not allowing you to sacrifice yourself for us. We'll figure out something else."

"I have to try."

"I'm still the captain of this ship, and you have to obey my orders."

"Listen to him," urged Nick.

Tatyana waved him off. "Captain, I'm not trying to be difficult, but so long as they're on board, they run the show. If they wanted to, they could ram this ship into anything they wanted, including one of those mega-liners. Our only option is to drive them off."

Fletcher locked his gaze on Tatyana as he ran through the options in his mind. After several seconds, he sighed. "I can't allow you to put yourself in such danger."

"Why?"

"Because it would be irresponsible. You might get killed."

"Would you send your crew into danger if the ship was sinking or on fire?"

"That's different. They're trained for emergencies."

"And I'm trained for this."

Fletcher began to speak but paused. He broke eye contact and stared over the bow.

"Captain," said Angelina. "I'm still unable to establish radio contact with land."

Tatyana softened her tone. "We don't have a choice."

Fletcher seemed in emotional pain. "I can't order a civilian to put her life in jeopardy for my ship."

"You're not." Tatyana smiled reassuringly. "I'm volunteering."

The captain spoke over his shoulder to Campbell. "How long before we reach that hurricane?"

"At this speed, less than two hours."

Fletcher hesitated.

"I'll make a deal with you," offered Tatyana. "It'll take me two hours to prepare. If in that time you can regain control of the ship or restore communications, we'll revisit the issue. If not, then I'm the last hope."

The captain finally gave in to the inevitable. "I assume you're ghost friend will be with you?"

Nick moved away from the windows and into the center of

the bridge. "You bet your ass I'll be there."

Tatyana flashed Nick a disapproving glare as she answered Fletcher. "Yes."

"Will you need any other help?"

"I could use at least one other person."

Giselle raised her hand. "I'll volunteer."

"No," Tatyana responded emphatically.

"Why?"

"Because they tried to kill you a few hours ago."

"All the more reason why I should be there. If..." Giselle swallowed. "If they're demanding a sacrifice, better me than one of you."

"You're not responsible for what happened to them. And you're not going to sacrifice yourself."

"Trust me. I don't want to die." Giselle forced a smile. "Consider me a distraction."

Nick nodded. "Her being there would take their attention off you."

"I'd still need a third person."

"Count me in." Angelina moved away from the console. "I know what to expect."

"Earlier this evening doesn't count."

"Maybe. But, after yourself, Miss Demarco and I have more experience with the supernatural than anyone else on board."

Tatyana could not argue with her logic or bravery. "I'm fine with it as long as the captain is."

Angelina glanced over at Fletcher. "Sir?"

"You have my permission."

"It's settled." Tatyana picked up her travel bag and slung it over her shoulder. "Giselle, Angelina, let's go back to my cabin and plan how we're going to do this. Captain, please let me know if there are any changes in the situation we should know about."

With that, the group headed back to Tatyana's stateroom.

✕　✕　✕

As Tatyana inventoried her supplies, she briefed Giselle and Angelina about the procedures she would perform during the cleansing, warned them what to expect in response from the spirits, and advised the women on what she required of them. Nick sat on the sofa, listening and offering advice when he felt it necessary. Nostradamus curled up on the sofa across the suite.

Tatyana repacked her tacky New Orleans travel bag and mumbled. "Shit."

"What is it?" asked Angelina.

"I wish I had more salt."

"What type of salt?"

"Kosher. Once they're expelled, it helps prevent them from returning."

"Would regular table salt do the trick?"

Tatyana thought for a moment. "It's better than nothing. Why do you ask?"

"We're still stocked for the maiden voyage. We have enough in storage for two thousand passengers for a week. Do you want me to have the crew bring it to the staff mess?"

"No. Have them take half to the engine room and the rest to where the rudder is."

"Can I use your phone?"

"Go ahead."

As Angelina made the call, Nick waved to catch Tatyana's attention. She joined him on the sofa.

"You look concerned," she said.

"I'm worried about the others. We're heading into a nightmare they're not prepared for. What will happen to them if they go gunning for blood? Especially Giselle."

"I don't know."

Tatyana sighed. She hated involving Giselle and Angelina

but had no other options. She and Nick could not do this alone, not two people against more than one hundred vengeful entities. They'd be overwhelmed. Even with the two inexperienced women, the odds remain more than twenty-nine to one, which still sucked. Maybe Angelina and Giselle would provide enough of a distraction so she and Nick could perform the cleansing, though Tatyana doubted that would work against so many spirits. Under normal circumstances, she would have researched how to perform mass cleansing effectively. Yet nothing about this situation was normal. Even worse, failure wouldn't mean someone's house would remain haunted this time. If Tatyana screwed up this one, she risked losing the ship and everyone on board.

No pressure, she tried to reassure herself.

Angelina hung up the phone and rejoined the others. "The salt is being sent to the engine room and steering."

"Good." Tatyana stood and slung the travel bag over her shoulder. "Let's prep those two areas first, then we'll head back to the staff mess."

✕　✕　✕

THE FIRST STOP was the engine room. Nostradamus and Nick watched from the sidelines as Tatyana performed her ritual and explained its significance to Giselle and Angelina. She laid a circle of table salt around the engines, then placed eight Selenite crystals equidistant around the circle, reciting the incantations after each procedure that would allow these metaphysical blocks to keep the spirits away once driven off. Due to the size of the space, the preparations took ninety minutes. Following the engine room, they made the same preparations to the steering room, which required half an hour. Though a long shot, Tatyana hoped that if they left the engine and steering areas to concentrate their energy in the staff mess, the captain could regain control and not lose it.

Halfway through setting up the protective barrier in the steering room, Tatyana felt the *Maria Doria* roll from one side to the other. She ignored the fear-driven emptiness that formed in the pit of her stomach, focusing instead on maintaining her balance and creating the protective circle. At the end of the procedure, while repacking the travel bag, she noticed the rolling had grown in severity.

"Is this normal?" Tatyana asked Angelina with a nonchalance that belied her growing anxiety.

"We're inside the hurricane."

"Will it get worse?"

"It's a Category Four. It's going to get a lot worse." Noticing Tatyana's fear, Angelina tried to sound comforting. "Don't worry. Cruise liners are built to withstand severe storms."

"You're just saying that to placate me."

"She's not," said Giselle. "We haven't lost a liner yet."

"Yet," teased Nick.

Tatyana ignored him.

"What next?" asked Angelina.

Tatyana took a deep breath. "Now we head for the staff—."

The ship's bow slowly rose several feet before suddenly dropping and leaning twenty degrees to starboard. Tatyana slid forward and to the right, reaching out at the last second and grabbing a pipe protruding from the bulkhead. The ship slowly righted itself.

"What the hell was that?"

"The captain turned the liner—"

"You mean the ghosts turned the liner," interrupted Giselle.

Angelina scowled at the woman. "Whoever is in charge of the ship turned into the waves so we could ride through them. It's standard procedure."

"What happens if you don't turn into the waves?"

Neither woman answered. The silence did nothing to decrease Tatyana's anxiety. Nick finally answered.

"If we're not heading into the waves, we could roll over."

Tatyana gasped. "You mean capsize?"

Angelina rolled her eyes. "Way to go, ghost boy. Scare your friend half to death."

Tatyana chuckled at the name. She would have to remember that.

However, with another lurch of the ship, her anxiety returned.

"Don't worry," comforted Angelina. "The crew who haunt this ship were all seasoned maritime personnel. They're in control and know what to do to keep us afloat."

"What if their goal is to bring us into the center of the storm and sink us?" asked Giselle.

The question caught Angelina off guard. Even Nick looked disturbed by that thought.

It worried Tatyana even more.

The ship lurched again. Nostradamus slid across the deck, his paws flailing to keep him upright. When things settled down, the dog raced over and cuddled against Tatyana's leg. She petted the dog's side to comfort him.

Angelina motioned toward Nostradamus. "You might want to consider taking him back to your stateroom where he'll be safe."

Tatyana usually kept Nostradamus by her side during investigations and cleansings. However, given the severity of the threat they faced, she agreed it would be better not to have him around. If the entities went after the dog, it would distract her attention when she needed to focus most.

"I agree with not taking him with us, but I don't want to leave him in the stateroom alone during the storm."

"What about bringing him to the bridge? They'll keep an eye on him."

"That'd be perfect. Thanks."

The trip back to the bridge was made difficult by the continued rocking motions of the liner. Tatyana and the others finally reached the bridge to discover they had been below so long the sun had risen. However, the layer of thick black and dark grey clouds from horizon to horizon prevented much light from filtering through. Fletcher stood at the front of the bridge, his eyes fixed across the bow. Tatyana went forward to talk with him. She gasped when she stepped beside the captain and leaned back against the console. For a moment, fear overcame all her senses.

Ahead of the *Maria Doria*, a series of waves rolled across the ocean's surface, each between fifty and seventy-five feet high. The liner's bow rose so high that Tatyana could not see the horizon. The ship hovered for a few seconds. Then, as the wave rolled past, the bow dropped into the trough and lurched precariously to the right. The next wave approached, filling the view from the bridge. It slammed into the submerging bow and splashed water across the windows. Several seconds passed before the water cleared away. The bow rose again as it crested the third wave, beginning the process again.

Tatyana blanched. Despite herself, she vomited on the deck.

"This is your first time at sea?" asked Fletcher.

Tatyana nodded, too scared and embarrassed to speak.

"It's terrifying the first time you go through it. After your third or fourth hurricane, it becomes boring."

"Th-this doesn't bother you?"

"Those things in control of the ship are following standard procedures. They're heading into the storm. We're in no danger."

Tatyana could not believe how Fletcher and his crew took this in stride.

Angelina joined them. "Sir, we're about to head down and exorcise the staff mess, but we wanted to leave the dog here on the bridge where he'll be safe."

"Permission granted."

As the two officers talked, Tatyana made her way over Nick, who stood on the wing, gazing longingly at the sea. Tatyana fought back the bile rising in her throat. "This doesn't make you seasick?"

"I'm a sailor. I love the ocean."

"Aren't you scared?"

Nick chuckled. "I went through a typhoon in 1944 far worse than this. It pounded the hell out of Task Force 38. Almost every ship made it through. This is nothing."

"'Almost every ship'?"

"Three foundered in the storm. But they were destroyers."

The *Maria Doria* dropped into another trough, and Tatyana hurled what remained in her stomach across the deck.

"Are you okay?"

"I'll be fine." Tatyana hacked, spitting up some vomitus.

Angelina and Giselle came up to them. The former asked, "Talking to Nick?"

"Yes."

The officer dropped two pills into Tatyana's hand. "Take these. They're Dramamine. They'll help with the sea sickness."

Tatyana popped them into her mouth and swallowed.

"Are you up to this?" asked Giselle. "You're as pale as a ghost. No pun intended."

"I am. When do you want to start?"

A wave slammed into the bridge window beside Tatyana, causing her to jump. She regained her composure and focused on the other women.

"No time like the present."

CHAPTER SIXTEEN

MAKING THEIR WAY down to the staff mess took longer than expected due to the incessant bucking of the liner. Rolling through each wave either knocked the women off balance or bounced them off the bulkheads. Being a veteran of life at sea, Angelina was used to such weather and moved about with ease. Tatyana felt like a martini being mixed in a cocktail shaker, with the added burden of lugging around her bag of cleansing supplies.

When they finally reached the staff mess, Nick stood outside waiting for them.

"Were you inside?" asked Tatyana.

"Yeah. You can definitely feel the malevolence in there, though it's only a loud hum at the moment. That'll change the moment you enter."

"Why?"

"They got angry when I entered. God knows what they would have done to me if I was corporeal. I walked around to get a feel of the spiritual tension but didn't engage them. They settled down after a few minutes. When you start the ritual, they'll probably go nuts."

"Damn. It's going to take several minutes to prepare the room, several minutes in which we'll be in danger."

"I can try and run interference for you while you set up." Nick's tone did not sound confident. Both remembered what Eliza had been able to do to him, and she was a single entity. This time they confronted one hundred and thirteen pissed-off entities.

"Are you talking with your friend?" asked Angelina.

Tatyana nodded. "He warned me they're agitated."

"Which means they'll be ready to pounce the minute we walk in." Giselle said it more as a statement than a question.

"I'm afraid so."

"What do you have to do before you can exorcise them?"

"The same procedures I did in the engine and steering compartments." The idea of being vulnerable to the spirits for that long did not settle well with Tatyana.

The *Maria Doria* pitched up, hovered, and dropped into the trough, nearly knocking the women off their feet.

"How well will your salt circle hold up to the ship's motion?" asked Angelina.

Shit. Tatyana had not considered that. Placing the bag on the floor, she removed a canister of sea salt and spread the contents along six feet of the corridor wall. The line held until the ship rolled to port, scattering the salt and breaking the line.

Angelina noticed the concerned expression on Tatyana's face. "I assume that's not good."

"If we can't circle the mess with a salt line, the spirits can return if they want to."

Giselle sighed. "That's not good."

"Even worse, the salt circle I'd create to protect you will be ineffective, putting both of you in jeopardy."

"It's a chance we'll have to take," offered Angelina.

Giselle said nothing.

Tatyana could not put them at such a risk. Without the salt circle to protect them, Giselle and Angelina would be vulnerable to the whim of the spirits and might easily wind up like Brendan. She could not live with their deaths on her conscious. Unless....

Reaching into the bag, she withdrew the box of Selenite crystals.

"How many pockets do you have?" she asked Angelina.

"Four."

Tatyana removed four stones and gave them to her. "Place one of these in each pocket."

"What are they?"

"Selenite crystals. They're powerful at warding off evil. Usually, you place them in the corners of the room where the spirit spends most of its time. They'll never stay in place in this storm, so you'll need to carry them on you."

As Angelina complied, Tatyana turned to Giselle. "And you?"

"Two."

She handed a pair of Selenite crystals to Giselle. As she placed the stones in her pockets, Tatyana did the same to herself and then recited the appropriate incantation.

"Your job is to protect these women against all spirits, benign and malevolent. You will not allow any spirits to harm them and, once this ship is cleansed, you are not to allow any spirits to attach themselves to these women. I know you'll do as I ask."

Tatyana then removed three canisters of sea salt from the bag. She opened one and stood in front of Angelina.

"I'm going to pour salt into the same pockets where you placed the stones."

Tatyana shook out salt into each pocket.

"Forgive me for getting personal."

Tatyana pulled open the front of Angelina's blouse and poured salt down the front.

"What's this for?" asked the officer.

"If I can't protect you within a circle of salt, giving you a coat of armor is the next best thing."

Tatyana yanked on Angelina's trousers and placed salt along her waist.

Angelina squirmed. "It's itchy."

"It's better than being dead," offered Nick as he watched intently.

Tatyana grinned. "Turn around."

Angelina complied. Tatyana poured salt down the back of her shirt and trousers.

"Close your eyes."

When Angelina did, Tatyana emptied the rest of the container across her head and shoulders. Tatyana then used the second and third containers of salt on Giselle and herself. Throwing the three cylinders back into the travel bag, she incited the next incantation.

"Your job is to protect these women from all spirits, benign and malevolent. You will not allow any spirits to harm them and, once this ship is cleansed, you are not to allow any spirits to attach themselves to these women. I know you'll do as I ask."

Tatyana removed a fourth container of salt and handed the bag to Angelina. "Once inside, I'm going to create a circle of salt around you two for protection."

"It won't last long," warned Angelina.

"I know. That's why I need you to constantly replenish the salt while I take on the spirits. Can you do that?"

"If it keeps us alive, sure." Angelina took a container of salt and raised the spout.

"Let's do this."

Tatyana opened the door to the staff mess. Angelina reached in and switched on the lights. All three women and Nick entered.

"*You're back.*" The voices of the hundred-plus spirits spoke in unison.

"We are." Tatyana stopped the others five feet from the door and formed a circle of salt around them.

"Your job is to protect these women from all spirits, benign and malevolent. You will not allow any spirits to harm them and, once this ship is cleansed, you are not to allow any spirits to attach themselves to these women. I know you'll do as I ask."

"*We're not certain if your courage or your stupidity blinds you. You realize that trying to banish us without fulfilling our wish will result in your deaths.*"

"What is your wish?" challenged Tatyana.

"*You already know that.*"

"Tell me again."

The voices spoke two words simultaneously—*justice* and *revenge*.

"I can give you justice."

The voices laughed sardonically. "*How?*"

"You showed me the horrors you went through. I know the wrong that was done to you. We'll make your suffering known to the world, have the corporation apologize, and make amends for how they mistreated your deaths."

"*It is not enough.*"

"Yes, it is. We'll correct the injustice."

"*Will you take this ship out of service and destroy it?*"

"No," said Giselle. "Corporate will never agree to that. It's too much of a financial loss."

Tatyana spun around and glared at her, the look of anger so intense it made Giselle avoid eye contact. Tatyana returned her attention to the spirits.

"I swear I'll do everything I can to set things right. I can also release you from this realm so you may all enjoy the afterlife."

"*What good is the afterlife to us?*" spat the voices. "*Our souls will spend infinity tormented by the knowledge that our lives were worth nothing here on Earth.*"

"She's only trying to help you." Nick stepped in front of Tatyana. "You don't want to be condemned for eternity because you took innocent lives in this realm."

The voices softened. "*We regret taking the life of the one called Brendan. We did it in a fit of rage.*"

"Then don't let your rage—"

"*Enough out of you.*" A circle of flame appeared above Nick. "*Your opinion is meaningless to us. You no longer remember what it is like to be bound to this plain of existence. Instead, you follow this woman and do her bidding like a puppy. Speak again and they will be your last words.*"

The circle of fire died out.

"*We are willing to go into the afterlife peacefully, but we require something first.*"

Tatyana allowed herself a glimmer of hope. "What?"

"*A sacrifice.*"

There goes the glimmer of hope. "What type of sacrifice?"

"*The one you call Giselle.*"

The woman sobbed.

"No!" Tatyana said defiantly.

"*She is no better than those who desecrated our resting place by raiding it for profit. She knew what had happened aboard the Caribbean Dream and kept it secret, hoping you would cleanse us without the truth ever coming to light. When her soul joins us, we will willingly enter the afterlife.*"

"I said no."

"*We need to prove that corporate cares about no one. One selfish life is a small price to pay to satisfy one hundred and thirteen tormented souls.*"

"One hundred and fourteen," said Nick. "You keep forgetting Branden."

Tatyana stepped closer to where the voice spoke. "I refuse."

"*Then you will all suffer. Everyone aboard this ship will die a horrible death.*"

"Not if I banish you from the *Maria Doria.*"

"*You are pathetic. We control this ship.*"

"I control you."

Another laugh came from the voices, this one filled with evil. "*We'll see about that.*"

The lights in the staff mess went out, plunging Tatyana and the others into darkness.

CHAPTER SEVENTEEN

F LETCHER KNEW SOMETHING was amiss the moment it occurred. The *Maria Doria* suddenly went quiet. Not that the liner had been making a lot of noise. There is a certain life to a ship at sea, such as the barely noticeable vibrations emanating from the engine. Most tourists and crew members never notice it. Fletcher did. To him, it was the heartbeat of the liner. Now it had ceased.

The mumbled f-bomb by Campbell confirmed the captain's worst fears.

"Sir, we've lost power."

"In what part of the ship?"

"I can't be certain, but I believe everywhere."

Which terrified Fletcher. He stepped over to the ECDIS console and lifted the phone. Silence. He punched in the number for the engine room. Nothing happened. The captain replaced the receiver.

"How long before the standby diesel generator switches on?" asked Campbell.

"It should be on by now." Fletcher turned to Hashimoto. "Miss Hashimoto."

"Sir?"

"Grab a radio and head down to the engine room. Check whether this power outage is isolated or throughout the ship. And find out how long it'll take to bring it back online."

"Right away."

The dread in her eyes expressed the fear everyone on the bridge felt over losing complete control of a vessel at sea during a hurricane. Grabbing a radio from the stand, Hashimoto tested it to make sure it connected to the captain's radio and bolted off the bridge.

Fletcher focused on the forward view. The liner's bow peaked a monstrous wave and hovered for several seconds, the bow dangling. Then the liner plunged into the trough. A moment later, the next wave crashed across the deck, throwing heavy sheets of water across the glass and along the outside decks. The *Maria Doria* began its tortuous assent up the next wave.

The captain glanced down at the console. Its bearing had already shifted one degree to port.

✕   ✕   ✕

HASHIMOTO MADE HER way into the engine room, the sudden tilt to port slamming her left arm and shoulder against the watertight hatch. A bolt of pain shot up her arm. She ignored it and searched for Sprague.

Hashimoto found the chief engineer in front of the electric control panel. Emergency lighting from overhead lamps barely lit it up. Five engineers stood around Sprague, shining flashlights on the panel or manuals they held, loudly arguing amongst themselves. Another engineer attempted to reset the non-fuse breakers in the distribution box without success. Hashimoto made her way over to the group.

"Sprague?"

He didn't acknowledge her.

"I need to know what the status is."

"Bugger off, mate. Can't you see we're busy?"

"Is that what you want me to tell the captain?"

"Tell the captain we have no bloody idea what's going on. The electricity went out for no apparent reason. The reset buttons don't bloody well work, and we have no indications why this wanker went down. And we can't get the standby generator running."

"What are you doing to fix it?"

Sprague rolled his eyes but never took his gaze off what he was doing. "We're following every emergency procedure listed in the bloody manual."

"Any idea how long it'll take?"

"It'll take a lot less time if I didn't have to answer so many bloody questions."

Hashimoto was about to chew off Sprague's head when the liner made its usual bucking motion as it rode the waves, only this time tilting to port a little too much. The ship groaned and righted itself, emitting the horrifying sound of steel being placed under tremendous stress.

Sprague turned to Hashimoto, his anger and frustration replaced by fear. "Tell the captain we're working on this as fast as possible and will let him know when we have anything further."

"I will." Hashimoto nodded at Sprague in solidarity. "Good luck."

"We're going to bloody need it."

Exiting the engine room, she keyed the radio.

"This is Fletcher."

"It's Hashimoto. I just talked to Sprague. He says the power is off throughout the ship, but they have no idea why. They're working on it now and will let you know."

"Thanks."

"Do you want me back on the bridge?"

"No. Head to steering. We have to get the rudder under our control if we hope to survive this storm."

"I'm on my way."

"WH-WHAT JUST HAPPENED?" Giselle stuttered.

"The lights went out," Angelina answered.

"No shit," retorted Tatyana.

A click sounded from the wall behind them and the emergency lights flicked on, barely illuminating the room.

Giselle looked around nervously. "Did the ghosts blow out the lights in here?"

"No. The whole ship lost power."

Tatyana gave her a quick glance. "How do you know?"

"Trust me. When you've been at sea so long as I have, you get to know when you're dead in the water."

Despite their situation, Tatyana chuckled. "Not a good choice of words."

"Dead in the water?"

Tatyana nodded.

"In this case, they're literal. The worst place to be in the middle of a hurricane is aboard a vessel that lost power. We're at the mercy of the storm with no way to start the engines or control the rudder."

Tatyana didn't want to know the answer to the next question. "What does that mean?"

"It means the waves will eventually push the *Maria Doria* until the ship isn't cutting through them but is parallel to them. When that happens, we run a good chance of capsizing."

"Or go down like the *Arvin*," warned Giselle.

Tatyana looked at the two women. "What happened to the *Arvin?*"

"The *Arvin* was a cargo freighter that broke in half during a bad storm off Turkey."

As if to emphasize the point, the *Maria Doria* crested a tall wave. The groaning of stressed steel echoed throughout the lower decks.

"In either case," added Nick, "even if the Coast Guard were here to help us, in this storm it'd be a miracle if a handful of us survived."

"*Now you get to endure what we went through,*" the voices spoke in unison. "*Adrift at sea with no way to control the ship and no one coming to help.*"

Tatyana stepped away from the others. "We always empathized with what you went through."

"*No one bothered to search for us. The crew of the Ise Maru never told the Coast Guard about the ship they collided with, so the Coast Guard never searched for us. We were left to die.*"

Giselle started to speak, but Tatyana waved for her to be silent. "We can't change what happened, but we can make amends, let the truth be told, and send you off to the afterlife."

"*We had no choice in our demise.*" The voices paused. "*But you do.*"

"What do you mean?"

"*Give us Giselle.*"

Giselle's face blanched. A shiver ran through her body.

"*What do you want with Giselle?*" demanded Tatyana.

The voices spoke as one but uttered two separate words—*justice* and *revenge*.

"It's not going to happen." Tatyana spoke as adamantly as possible.

"*Give us the one we desire, and we'll return full control of your ship back to you.*"

"And if we don't?"

The voices grew deeper and more menacing. "*Then everyone aboard the Maria Doria will die at sea as we did. Sacrificing one life to spare many is not bad, especially when that person helped perpetuate this indignity against us. We never had such an option.*"

Giselle moved toward the edge of the salt circle. "If that's what it takes—"

Tatyana rushed over and prevented the woman from crossing the boundary. "If you step over that line, I can't protect you." She spun around to face the shimmering form of the entity. "As for you, what happened to all of you was tragic and horrific, but it was an accident. I refuse to let you take an innocent life to satisfy your lust for vengeance."

A spike in the level of malevolence filled the staff mess. Tatyana felt it tingling through her body.

"*We do not seek justice/revenge for the accident that took our lives. We seek justice/revenge for the indignity that befell us afterward. For the fact that the company we perished for decided to defile our souls by ransacking the vessel we died on to build this ship."*

Nick moved up alongside her. "Be careful. You're pissing them off."

"I understand your suffering, but—"

"You do not understand anything about how badly we suffered." For the first time, the combined voices of the spirits spoke with anger and hatred in their tone.

"You're right," Tatyana said humbly. "I can't change the past. But I can release your souls and end your suffering."

"The same thing will happen after we get what we demand."

Screw it, thought Tatyana. There was no reasoning with them. "I will not allow you to take an innocent life."

The sardonic laugh that emanated from the apparition made Tatyana's blood run cold. *"Innocent? You're a fool. That woman knew about what happened to us, how the location of our last moments on earth had been defiled, and purposefully kept it from you to protect those that perpetrated this indignity. Not only did she attempt to cover this up and perpetuate our suffering, but by not being honest, she endangered the lives of everyone aboard this ship."*

"You're endangering our lives," snapped Tatyana. "You killed a man who had nothing to do with your deaths. Burned him alive as you had been. Giselle may have taken away your eternal rest. I can fix that. But you murdered an innocent man, and he can't be brought back to life."

"Enough!" the combined voices bellowed. *"We are through talking. You mean nothing to us. That woman is the one we want. Once we have justice/revenge, we will depart this ship. Will you step aside and let us do what we must?"*

"No."

"So be it. Then we'll go through you."

A ring of fire five feet in circumference formed between Tatyana and the apparition. With a flick of the latter's hand, it flew toward Tatyana.

CHAPTER EIGHTEEN

NICK SENSED THE sudden surge of anger and hatred. He had only seconds to react.

His first reaction was to protect Tatyana, his friend and the one person he truly cared about. That gave way to common sense. As much as he cared for Tatyana, she knew how to handle herself in such situations, whereas Giselle and Angelina were helpless. Years of military training kicked in. In a crisis, you protect those who need help the most.

As the ring of fire formed in the center of the staff mess, Nick ran over and stood in front of Giselle and Angelina.

✕ ✕ ✕

FLETCHER SWITCHED HIS attention between the storm battering the *Maria Doria* and the security camera monitor for the staff mess. Because of the blackout, the console monitor on the bridge did not function, so he had no idea what was happening in the staff mess. The captain could not get what had happened to Brandon off his mind. He had promised Tatyana he would not interfere with her cleansing but, as captain, he could not sit by and do nothing.

Removing the radio from his pocket, he keyed the microphone and called his chief of security. "Mr. Michaels, this is Captain Fletcher. Do you read me?"

"Michaels here."

"I need you to send a security team down to the staff mess. Make sure fire-fighting and medical units are with them."

"Did we have another incident?"

"No. But I want to be ready in case—"

Campbell called out to Fletcher. The terrified tone of his voice warned the captain that something terrible was about to happen. Fletcher glanced down at the monitor, but it was still not operating. He raised the radio to his mouth to order Michaels to hurry when Campbell tapped the captain on the shoulder.

"Sir, I'm referring to that." Campbell pointed through the front windows.

Fletcher followed the officer's finger and muttered a single word.

"Shit."

A wave fifty feet high roared toward the starboard bow of the *Maria Doria*, which was already at a dangerous angle due to the liner's lack of control. This wave came in at a slight angle to the other waves generated by the storm. Fletcher watched for five terrifying seconds as it raced toward them, striking the bow at a forty-five-degree angle.

The *Maria Doria* listed precariously to port.

✕ ✕ ✕

INSIDE THE STAFF mess, the entity launched the ring of fire at Tatyana. A sudden lurch of the ship threw her and the other women against the port bulkhead. Tatyana slammed against the steel, the force of the impact knocking the wind out of her and momentarily stunning her. She felt the flames drawing near. Thankfully, the unexpected movement threw off the apparition's aim. The ring of fire slammed into the bulkhead three feet above Tatyana's head and fizzled out, the residual heat scorching Tatyana's hair and burning the back of her neck.

Tatyana regained her senses and looked around, assessing the situation. The apparition hovered in the same spot from where it had attacked her. Giselle and Angelina lay against the bulkhead a few feet to her right. Angelina was unconscious, her body slumped to one side. Giselle winced from the pain. Nick remained standing where he had taken a defensive position in front of the others. Salt lay spread across the deck, the circle broken by the sudden lurch. Nothing remained to protect Giselle and Angelina.

"Are you alright?" Tatyana asked as the ship slowly righted itself.

"Angelina is out cold," huffed Giselle. "And I broke my right arm."

"Where's the salt container?"

"I don't know."

Tatyana searched the room. The travel bag with her gear had slid across the deck and sat against the bulkhead five yards from Giselle. There was no way to protect them now.

"Nick...."

"I'm on it." He shifted position toward the bulkhead, blocking the two women.

Tatyana stood. Her back ached from slamming into the steel and her scalp and neck burned.

The apparition moved toward Giselle.

✕　✕　✕

"CAPTAIN," IAN'S VOICE came over the radio. "Do you still want me to send a security team to the staff mess?"

Fletcher quickly assessed the situation. The rogue wave pushed aside the *Maria Doria* until it was almost parallel with the oncoming waves. One slammed into the starboard beam of the liner, tilting it to port and pushing it aside. The groans of straining steel echoed throughout the vessel. Fletcher spun around and peered out toward the stern. Though barely perceptible, like the swaying of a skyscraper in the wind, he saw the liner bend slightly amidships under the strain. They could not be in a worse situation. With no ability to steer the liner, the ship was at the mercy of the waves slamming against the hull. The chances were good that this continued pounding would eventually capsize the *Maria Doria,* or worse, break her in half.

"Captain, are you there?"

In a matter of seconds, the lives of the three women in the staff mess paled to the safety of his crew. Fletcher keyed the talk button on the radio.

"Belay that last order. Prepare to abandon ship."

✕   ✕   ✕

ANOTHER RING OF fire formed in front of the apparition.

Giselle rolled over and covered Angelina with her body to protect the unconscious woman from the impending inferno.

Tatyana struggled to her feet and limped across the deck. With the salt circle broken and nothing else available to ward off the spirits, she opted for a Hail Mary play.

"By the good within the spirit world and the holiness of the religious realm, I demand that you leave this ship at once and—"

"*Enough!*"

A blast of energy shot out from the apparition. It passed through Nick, leaving him untouched. The force knocked Giselle off Angelina and threw Tatyana back against the bulkhead, pinning the three women against the wall. None of them could move.

"*We are tired of this. We seek only what is rightfully ours.*"

The apparition floated toward Giselle.

✕   ✕   ✕

ANTONIO MARTINETTI, THE chief mechanic, rushed around the confines of the steering gear department, a task made all the more difficult by having only a flashlight to see combined with the liner's bucking and rolling. He frantically checked every aspect of the rudder to determine why it failed. Everything seemed to be functioning properly. The amount, temperature, and pressure of the hydraulic oil were fine. No hydraulic oil or grease leaked from the cylinders or bearings. According to the sounding pipe, no water had made its way into the rudder trunk. Even though the liner had lost power, manual steering should be operable, yet it would not function for some reason.

The radio attached to his belt came to life. "Martinetti, this is the captain. What's the progress on restoring rudder control?"

Martinetti keyed the talk button. "I have no idea what's going on. There's nothing mechanically wrong with the steering mechanism, yet it won't respond. It's almost as if the damn ship refuses to cooperate."

"Keep on it," ordered Fletcher. "If you can't get it back under our control, we'll capsize in this storm."

The radio went dead. Martinetti reattached it to his belt.

No pressure at all, he thought.

✕ ✕ ✕

NICK STEPPED CLOSER to the apparition, blocking its path. "And what is rightfully yours? Revenge and justice?"

"*Yes*." The apparition glowed with a reddish hue.

"And you're willing to put the lives of over a hundred sailors at risk to fulfill that desire?"

The apparition paused. Its hue changed back to a soft, mellow white. The ring of fire dissipated. The apparition studied Nick, their head tilted to one side as they processed the unusual entity before them. After a few moments, the flickering of multiple images of the deceased crew stopped. One image remained constant, that of a dignified, older man with a white beard who wore a captain's uniform.

"*I'm Captain Robert Schreiner of the Caribbean Dream. Who are you?*"

"Nick Thompson."

"*You wear the uniform of a naval officer. Did you die in combat?*"

"No. I survived several campaigns in World War II and was murdered by my wife when I returned home and found her cheating on me."

A look of pain and understanding flashed across the spectral image's face. "*What are you doing here?*"

"I'm with that young woman." Nick motioned toward Tatyana. "She's a paranormal investigator and is here to set your souls free so you can move on to the afterlife."

"*We will leave once we get justice/revenge for the disservice done to us.*"

"Like I said, are you willing to sacrifice over a hundred of your fellow sailors to achieve that goal?"

The image of Captain Schreiner stiffened. "*What do you mean?*"

"You took control of the ship, steered us into a hurricane, and cut all power to the vessel. Without any way to control the liner, everyone on board will be dead within minutes."

As if to emphasize the point, the liner listed sharply to port, hovered at a dangerous angle for a few seconds, and slowly righted itself.

"You'll get your vengeance on that woman, but at what cost? The people who decided to use material from the *Caribbean Dream* will never see justice. And the cost will be the sacrifice of over a hundred men and women just like you who don't deserve to die the same as you. Do you think your souls will truly be at peace with that haunting your conscience?"

The apparition resumed flickering, showing the face of each of the condemned crew members in rapid succession. Each bore an expression of sadness, guilt, or shame.

The lights inside the staff mess turned on.

✕   ✕   ✕

THE ECDIS CONSOLE on the bridge lit up.

"Captain," yelled Campbell. "We have power."

Thank God, thought Fletcher. But he would express his gratitude later.

"Hard right rudder and full speed ahead."

Campbell had initiated the moves before the captain ordered them. The rogue wave bore in on the *Maria Doria*, only a few hundred feet away and closing rapidly. Fletcher gripped the console until the knuckles on his hands turned white. He held his breath and prayed, invoking every deity he could think of to save his vessel and crew, as the bow of the liner slowly arched toward the incoming wave. A part of him knew they would never make it.

Nostradamus moved alongside the captain, leaned into his leg, and whined. Fletcher reached down and petted him.

"It'll be over soon, boy."

They were at a fifteen-degree angle when the wave hit the *Maria Doria*. The bow disappeared beneath the surface and the liner tilted precariously to port. A wall of water slammed against the bridge, hanging there for several seconds. Fletcher waited for the inevitable capsizing and for the liner to begin its long, slow plunge to a watery grave.

A moment later, the water flowed off the windows. The *Maria Doria* sat in the trough between two waves, miraculously righting itself, cutting its way through the choppy sea and beginning its rise up the next wave.

Nostradamus glanced up at the captain, confusion in his eyes.

Fletcher smiled at the dog and scratched behind his ears. "We're going to make it, boy."

Nostradamus wagged his tail.

THE FINAL LURCH of the liner terrified Nick, not so much as what it meant for him but for the lives of all those aboard. After a few seconds, he felt the *Maria Doria* resume its tortured ride through the storm. The going for the next few hours would be rough, but at least they would make it.

"Thank you." Nick spoke softly.

"*Forgive us,*" the multiple voices pleaded as one. "*We realized not what we had become.*"

Tatyana limped up beside Nick. "Are you ready to be sent on to eternal peace?"

"*We do not deserve it.*"

"Yes, you do."

The apparition bowed its head.

"I call on the kindness of the good spirits to guide these tortured souls off this vessel and to a well-deserved and peaceful afterlife. I call upon the holy spirits to forgive these souls of their sins, offer them redemption, and allow them into your realm. May the grace of all that is good and holy be with them."

The apparition slowly degraded, becoming a mist that filtered through the ceiling of the staff mess and began its long journey elsewhere. Just before it dissipated, the image of Captain Schreiner appeared one final time. He nodded toward Nick and saluted the junior officer. Nick returned the gesture. The captain mouthed the words "thank you" as the spectral image disappeared.

Nick sighed, an unusual gesture for a ghost. "I can't believe we did it."

"You did it. If we relied on me, we'd all be joining them in Davey's Jones gym locker."

Nick did not correct Tatyana. Instead, he turned to her and grinned.

"Come on. Let's get you and the girls to sickbay."

CHAPTER NINETEEN

WITH THE LINER now under his control, Fletcher sent a security team down to the staff mees to check on Tatyana and the others. Finding Angelina still unconscious and the other two women in pain, the team brought all three to the sick bay where the ship's doctor, Doc Fried, examined them. Given what they had gone through, they were fortunate. Angelina suffered the most, the crash against the bulkhead causing a slight fracture to her skull and giving her a severe concussion, which would take her out of commission for four to six weeks. Giselle had severely bruised her left shoulder during the liner being tossed about and had broken her collar bone when the entity slammed her against the wall. Compared to the other two, Tatyana fared well—she suffered deep tissue bruising to her left shoulder and upper back muscles, as well as first-degree burns to the back of her scalp and neck, nothing that a few pain relievers, some antibiotic cream, and some physical therapy wouldn't cure.

Once the hurricane let up, Fletcher came down to the sick bay to check on them. He brought along Nostradamus. On seeing Tatyana, the dog rushed over to the bed, placed his front paws on the mattress, and gave his mistress a face bath. The captain allowed himself a smile at the display of affection.

Fletcher stepped over to the beds. "Good morning."

"It's morning already?" asked Tatyana.

"It's almost ten o'clock. Doc sent up a medical report earlier today on your conditions. I wanted to see how you ladies are doing."

"I'm alive." Giselle motioned with her head toward the cast on her shoulder, wincing as she did. "The doc put in some pins to hold the fractured bones in place. And I have to wear this thing on my neck until the bone mends."

"Is it that bad?"

"It's uncomfortable and restrictive."

"Not as restrictive as having your soul condemned to an ocean liner."

Giselle broke eye contact and lowered her head.

Fletcher turned to Angelina. "Miss Rosario?"

Doc Fried walked past the captain and stood by Angelina's bed. "She's not allowed to talk for a few days. I want to let her brain rest. The concussion is pretty bad."

"Will she be all right?" asked the captain, genuinely concerned.

"I don't foresee any complications. She needs to rest for a while to recover fully."

Fletcher nodded and shifted his attention back to Angelina. "Miss Rosario, take all the time you need. I've already wired a sitrep back to the home office and told them that, when you recover, I want you transferred back to whichever ship I've been assigned to."

Angelina grinned and nodded ever so slightly.

"Whichever ship?" asked Tatyana. "Does that mean that the *Maria Doria* will be decommissioned?"

"That's up to corporate. I have no say in the matter. But I assume the liner will at least be taken out of service for a while and the crew transferred to different ships." Fletcher moved alongside Nostradamus, scratching the dog on the top of its head as he talked to Tatyana. "And I owe you a major debt of thanks."

"For cleansing the ship?"

"For sending the souls of our comrades to the afterlife."

"That was Nick. He convinced them to leave."

"Is Nick your ghost friend?"

Tatyana nodded. "He's a naval officer from World War II."

"That makes sense. Only those of us who have spent time out here understand how tough life at sea can be. Months spent away from loved ones. And so many of us die horrible deaths alone without closure for our families. I doubt those who lost someone aboard the *Caribbean Dream* even knew what happened."

"Do you think Miami Cruise Lines will ever tell them the truth?"

"Doubtful." The captain's expression changed to one of disgust mixed with disappointment. "But I will."

Giselle's eyes widened. "Corporate isn't going to like that."

"Screw corporate. The families deserve the truth."

Tatyana grew concerned. "You're not going to tell them everything that happened on board the *Maria Doria*?"

"Not all the details. Just that you contacted the souls of those lost aboard the *Caribbean Dream* and that they live peacefully in the afterlife."

"Good for you."

"Thanks. Now, if you'll excuse me, I have to get back to the bridge. Arrangements have been made to fly you back to New Hampshire, and your payment has been deposited into your bank account. If you need anything in the meantime, just let me know."

"I will. And thank you."

"No, thank you." Fletcher exited sick bay, leaving Nostradamus with his mistress.

Tatyana scratched Nostradamus behind the ears for a few more minutes before telling him to lie down. The dog curled up beside her bed. Tatyana leaned back and settled in. She wanted to sleep for a while.

She had something important to do before the liner returned to New Orleans.

✕   ✕   ✕

TATYANA OPENED THE door to the staff mess and stepped inside. Nick and Nostradamus followed. The three stopped inside the room.

"I don't detect any spectral auras," said Tatyana. "Do you?"

Nick closed his eyes and listened for a few seconds. "Nothing. Not even a background hum. None of the spirits remained behind."

Nostradamus walked away and sniffed everything he came across, more intent on checking out the new surroundings than detecting any spectral residue.

Tatyana glanced around the room. No one had picked up yet after last night's cleansing. Granules of salt lay scattered across the floor along with several empty salt containers and her travel bag of supplies. She stepped over to the bag, hefted it onto one of the mess tables, and pulled aside the flaps. Thankfully, nothing had fallen out.

"Do you think this is necessary?" Nick looked around. "All the souls passed on to another realm."

"Probably not. But establishing barriers so they can never return is part of the process."

"Are you doing this for Giselle?"

Tatyana chuckled. "No. This is something I must do for Captain Schreiner and the others. Do you want to help me?"

"I wish I could. But I'll gladly keep you company."

Tatyana and Nick circled the mess staff and kitchen, the former laying down a barrier of salt where the walls met the floor. She could only carry three containers due to her injury and had to go back several times to retrieve more salt from her bag. When finished, Tatyana recited the incantation asking the salt to prevent any spirits, benign or malevolent, from returning to this space. She then followed the same procedures with

Selenite crystals, placing them in the corners of the staff mess and kitchen, where possible concealing the crystals from view so they would not be removed. Finally, she deployed a barrier of olive oil across each entranceway and used the oil to form a cross on each door as another ward to keep them away.

Given her pain, it took Tatyana several hours to complete everything. When finished, she sat in one of the booths and leaned back against the cushions. Nick sat across from her. Nostradamus curled up on the floor and napped.

"I hate to disappoint you," said Nick. "You know the crew will clean this up and undo everything?"

"I know. I'll tell the captain to give this place a week before anyone uses or cleans it. Hopefully, that'll give time for the effects of the preventions to take hold."

"What now? Drinks on the Lido Deck?"

"No way. After the past few days, I'll never set foot on a ship again. I'm going back to my cabin and rest until we dock."

"Then it's too boring for me." Nick stood. "I'll check in with you once you get back to your place."

"Okay. And Nick." Tatyana reached out to take his hand, stopping when she realized the futility of the gesture. "Thanks."

"I didn't do anything."

"Yes, you did. You saved Giselle and Angelina. And you were the one who convinced Schreiner and the others to leave without demanding revenge. I could never have done that. The three of us... hell, everyone aboard this ship... would probably be dead if it weren't for you."

"You're welcome. I'm glad I could finally be of help."

"What do you mean? I couldn't do this without you." Then she added. "And I still hate being at sea."

Nick smiled. If he had been able to, Tatyana felt he would have blushed. Instead, he merely waved, morphed into a mist, and dissipated.

Tatyana reached over and patted Nostradamus on the side. "Come on, boy. Let's go back to the cabin."

✕   ✕   ✕

AN AMBULANCE HAD been waiting for Angelina when the *Maria Doria* docked in New Orleans and rushed her to the Tulane Medical Center. A limousine picked up Tatyana, Nostradamus, and Giselle an hour later. No one saw them off, the entire crew being too busy. The only one who spoke with them was the driver who offered the usual pleasantries as he loaded their luggage. Once everyone was aboard, the driver closed the limo and headed for the airport.

As they pulled away, Tatyana leaned forward and studied the *Maria Doria* as it receded in the distance. It looked so peaceful, like every other cruise ship lined up along the dock ready to take thousands of tourists on an over-priced pleasure cruise. She wondered if the *Maria Doria* would ever be taken out of service or eventually slipped back in with the other liners. If the latter, would anyone other than herself and a handful of people know what truly happened?

Sadly, Tatyana knew the answer to those questions, and it infuriated her.

Giselle rested in the seat across from her, a sling holding her right arm to allow the collarbone to mend. The woman seemed upset, though Tatyana could not determine why. Was it shock over what she had gone through and nearly losing her life, which would only be natural? Frustration over dealing with corporate? Or embarrassment because she would have to tell Tatyana that nothing would be done regarding the recent incidents? After what they had gone through, Tatyana had a right to know.

"Have you heard what your bosses plan to do with the *Maria Doria*?"

"Knowing them, they'll advertise it as a haunted cruise ship and sell paranormal tours."

Tatyana was taken aback by the woman's honesty. "You

gotta be kidding."

"Maybe that's an exaggeration, but I'll be shocked if corporate doesn't place her back in service within a few months."

"Did you tell them yet what happened?"

"I did," Giselle answered a bit defensively. Then her tone softened. "I haven't written up my official report, but I talked to corporate earlier today by radio and filled them in on everything. They sounded skeptical, though I couldn't tell if that's because they didn't believe me or didn't want the true story being known."

"What will Fletcher and the rest of the crew say in their reports?"

"I believe the captain when he says he'll contact the relatives of the deceased and tell them that their souls are in a better place. Fletcher's a good man. As for the others, who knows? Anybody who goes against corporate risks being fired and blacklisted within the industry."

"Including you?"

Giselle grimaced and nodded.

"Does that mean you'll also cave in?"

For a moment, Giselle bristled. Tatyana prepared for an argument. The woman calmed down and avoided eye contact.

"I understand why you feel that way considering I hid the details of the *Caribbean Dream* from you. I'm not taking this lightly, especially since the ghosts wanted me as their sacrificial lamb, and the rest of you protected me at the risk of your own lives. I promise I'll push to have the *Maria Doria* decommissioned, but...."

"But you doubt corporate will take the financial loss."

"Exactly. I'll spin it to them as an acceptable loss, telling them the tax credit we'll get sending the liner to be taken apart will be far less than the public relations hit we'll suffer if word of what happened leaked. With the right mixture of greed and common sense, hopefully they'll do the right thing, even if it's for all the wrong reasons. At the very least, I'll push for corporate to gut the staff mess and replace it with new appliances. I'm not hopeful."

An awkward silence filled the limo until they arrived at Louis Armstrong International Airport. The driver made his way to the private section of the airport, pulled up alongside a Gulfstream G280, parked, and climbed out to retrieve Tatyana's bags from the trunk.

"I take it you're not flying back to New England with me?" asked Tatyana.

"Doc Fried didn't want me to escort you to the airport. Said I needed to get to the hospital ASAP. I ignored her. Considering all you did for us, this was the least I could do."

"I appreciate it."

The driver opened the door and stuck his head inside. "Are you ready, Miss Madison?"

Nostradamus jumped out of the limo, rubbing against the driver and covering his black trousers with fur, although the driver didn't seem to care. Tatyana followed when Giselle stopped her.

"By the way, I paid you the rest of your fee, plus a twenty percent gratuity."

"Thank you."

"It's my pleasure." Giselle smiled at her friend. "Your job is a lot more dangerous than mine."

The driver helped Tatyana out of the car, closing the door behind her, and then carried her luggage aboard the jet. The flight attendant met her at the bottom of the ramp, smiling and shaking her hand. He practically yelled over the noise of the engines warming up.

"Good afternoon, Miss Reynolds. I'm Sergei. I'll be taking care of you on your flight home. If you'll follow me, please."

Sergei led Tatyana to her seat. Nostradamus jumped into the one opposite her.

"We'll be taking off in a few minutes so we don't lose our place in line. Once we're airborne, can I bring anything for you and your dog?"

"Nostradamus will be fine. I'll have a Sazerac."

"Let me see if we have the ingredients. Right now, I must ask you to fasten your seatbelts. The pilot will let you know when it's okay to roam around the cabin."

As Tatyana complied, Sergei lifted and secured the ramp, prepared the cabin for take-off, and strapped himself in. Less than fifteen minutes later, the jet lifted off the runway and began its flight back to New England. Tatyana watched out the side window until New Orleans passed from view.

The aircraft's intercom came on. "Miss Reynolds, this is your captain. We've reached our cruising altitude, so feel free to unfasten your seatbelt. Sergei will be around in a few minutes with your drink order. If there's anything you need, please let one of us know. Other than that, enjoy your flight."

Tatyana glanced over at Nostradamus. "So, boy. What did you think of that last adventure?"

The dog remained curled up on the seat and sighed, his jowls making a fluttering sound as he did.

"I know. It was bad. The worst cleansing I've encountered so far. Maybe I'm in over my head. Do you think I should give up my paranormal investigations before one of us gets hurt, or worse?"

Nostradamus raised his head and stared at Tatyana.

"Do you think that's a good idea?"

Nostradamus tilted his head to one side and whined.

"No?" Tatyana leaned back against her seat and thought out loud. "Yeah, you're probably right. I'd miss it. Except for this past time, Salem, and Kathleen, it's been fun. I enjoy helping those having to deal with ghosts and sending lost spirits on their way. Maybe I should continue, just pass on taking dangerous jobs for a while. What do you think?"

The dog tilted his head in the opposite direction.

"I know you don't understand me, but I'll let you decide. Bark once if you think I should give up paranormal investigating entirely or twice if you think I should continue but just take on normal cases for a while."

Nostradamus perked up. His tail wagged with frenetic energy. The dog lifted his head and barked once. Then again.

Tatyana chuckled. "It's settled. We continue our investigations and avoid cases someone will make into a book or movie. Do you agree?"

Nostradamus jumped off the seat and came over to Tatyana. He barked once, then placed his chin on her knee, begging to be petted. Tatyana obliged, sending his tail wagging again.

A few minutes later, Sergei entered the cabin holding a tray with a tumbler and a dog biscuit. He stopped by Tatyana and placed the drink on her table.

"You were in luck. We had everything needed to make a Sazerac. I hope you enjoy it." Then, in a conspiratorial whisper, "I went a little heavy on the alcohol."

"Thank you."

Tatyana sipped the drink. Sergei wasn't kidding. He went more than a little heavy on the alcohol. Not that she would complain. After the past few days, she needed it.

"This is fantastic."

"I'm glad you like it. We have enough ingredients for another two drinks."

"I'll probably take you up on those."

Sergei held up the biscuit. "Is it okay if your dog has this?"

Nostradamus spun around and sat, his eyes switching between Sergei and the treat.

Tatyana grinned. "Yes."

Sergei offered the dog the treat. Nostradamus snatched it out of the Russian's hand and, his tail still wagging, ran around behind Tatyana's seat where he proceeded to devour his snack.

The Russian stepped back a pace. "Is there anything else I can get you, ma'am?"

Tatyana thought for a moment, feeling relaxed and content.

"Thank you, Sergei. I'm fine for the moment."

PREVIEW OF
THE CHRONICLES OF PAUL II:
ERRAND OF MERCY

P AUL MADISON SLOWLY emerged from a deep slumber.
Without opening his eyes, he shifted his body in the love
seat and rolled his neck from one side to the other. The
snapping and crackling of the muscles warned him he would be
sore after last night. A bright light on his face told him the sun
had risen, though he could not tell if it was early morning or
late afternoon, and as such, he had no idea how long he had
slept. Not that it mattered. Paul felt as exhausted as when he
fell asleep the previous evening, only now without the adrenalin
rush from spending several hours battling the living dead. He
definitely could use—

A loud noise came from the other room. Paul bolted upright and felt in his lap for the Vepr-12 semiautomatic shotgun.
It lay propped up against the love seat's arm on the right. The
knit comforter he had covered himself with remained across his
legs and chest, but someone had come down during the night
and covered his shoulders with a wool blanket. Probably
Daphne. The thought made him smile.

The loud noise broke the silence again. Only it was not
human screams or the moaning of the living dead, but
laughter. It came from the kitchen. Then he smelled the
enticing aroma of eggs, bacon, and sausage. And coffee.
Freshly-brewed coffee. For a second, Paul thought the last two
days had been a bad dream until he glanced down and noticed
his gore-splattered clothes. The others must be having breakfast, enjoying a few moments of the last vestiges of humanity.
He could not blame them. It sounded awesome. He only hoped
they had saved him some.

Paul pulled the comforter and blanket off him, balled them up, and dropped them on the floor beside the loveseat. He groaned as he stood, every muscle in his body protesting. Hopefully, the owners of this place had left some Tylenol upstairs. Once on his feet, he stretched and turned his body, the cracking of his muscles even more pronounced than before. Shouldering the Vepr, he made his way to the kitchen.

The rest of his group sat around the table, chatting and enjoying the first decent meal any of them had eaten in two days. Daphne sat with her back to him. The two of them had been together since zero hour of the outbreak when he rescued her from deaders in Pittsburgh. Together, they had fought their way from central Pennsylvania to the east coast of Maryland, saving the other members of the team along the way. She wore the same outfit she had on when he saved her—jeans, dress boots, circular glasses, and an orange sweater that tightly fit her well-endowed chest.

Akiko and Toshii sat at the long edge of the table to Daphne's right. He and Daphne had rescued the mother and son from an Exxon service station in Brownsville, where they were hiding after being attacked by deaders. The father had been killed protecting his family. The brindle-colored Boxer curled up underneath Toshii's chair. Toshii had named it Gojira. They had adopted the dog—or more precisely, the dog had adopted them—after pulling a deader off during the rescue of Akiko and Toshii.

Unfortunately, they had also picked up Sparky, the cowardly, selfish asshole who owned the service station. Sparky had proven more of a liability than anything else. Paul had wanted to leave him behind on several occasions but didn't, letting his humanity get the better of him. He regretted that decision last night while crossing the Chesapeake Bay Bridge. To save himself, Sparky had shoved Rebecca Daniels out of the way, sending the poor woman to her death. Paul corrected his mistake by using Sparky as deader bait so the rest of the group could escape.

Ed Daniels stood in front of the stove, scrambling eggs in one pan and broiling sausage links and bacon in another. Ed and Rebecca had saved the others when deaders had surrounded them on Route 119 east of Point Marion, Pennsylvania. None of them would have made it this far if not for Ed's Suburban. In return for helping them out, Rebecca had lost her life. For someone whose wife had died last night, not because of deaders but due to the selfish act of an asshole, Ed seemed to be holding it together well, although that was probably for show.

And finally, Lisa, the pretty young blonde Paul had rescued from the limousine as they crossed the Chesapeake Bay Bridge. Last night, she had worn a rain-drenched red dress and had discarded her high heels. Now she wore jeans, a white shirt, and sneakers raided from upstairs.

On seeing Paul, Gojira lifted his head and barked once. Daphne grabbed the .38 off the table and spun around in her chair, aiming it at Paul. He stepped back and raised his hands.

"I'm not one of those things."

"Sorry. Just jittery." Daphne placed the gun down on the table. She broke into a flirtatious smile. "I'm glad to see you're finally awake."

"What do you mean?" He pointed to the stove. "You're having breakfast."

"It's brunch," chuckled Ed. "It's almost ten in the morning. Want some?"

"Yes. I haven't had a good meal in days."

Lisa held up a mug with steam flowing from the top. "Hot coffee."

"Even better. But I still want some eggs and sausage."

"Coming right up."

Paul went over to the coffee maker, poured himself a mug, and returned to the table. Daphne patted the empty chair beside her. When he sat down, she placed a hand on his back and tenderly rubbed his shoulder.

"What were you talking about when I came in?"

Toshii looked up from his plate. "We were trying to figure out what happened to Ian."

Shit, Paul chastised himself. How could he have forgotten about Ian, the Boy Scout they picked up in Griffin after he jumped to safety from a bridge engulfed by flames?

"The last time I saw him was before we crossed the bridge," said Akiko. "He helped Toshii and me out of the car. We never saw him after that."

"Ed and I don't recall seeing him on the bridge," added Daphne. "We thought maybe he had helped you save Lisa."

"I don't recall seeing anyone but you until we rejoined the others." Lisa reached out and patted Paul on the hand. "By the way, thanks. I'd still be trapped in that limo if it wasn't for you."

Daphne bristled. She slid her hand under the table and massaged Paul along his inner thigh. "Do you remember seeing him?"

"No. I was the last one to climb the suspension cable. If Ian had been on the bridge with us, I would have seen him."

Akiko bowed her head. "Poor boy."

"Hopefully, he went quickly." Ed slid three scrambled eggs and three link sausages on a plate and placed it in front of Paul.

An awkward silence followed. Paul stared at his plate, embarrassed that he had forgotten about Ian. Finally, Ed tapped him on the shoulder.

"Eat up. That's the last of it. There was no sense letting it sit in the fridge to rot."

That's true, thought Paul. They were in a new, terrifying world where death was common. His group would more than likely lose a lot more people before this ended. He said a silent prayer for Ian and then dug into his meal.

"Where do we go from here?" asked Daphne. "We lucked out that there are no deaders nearby, but we can't stay here forever. Annapolis is on the other side of these woods. I'm surprised they haven't found us already."

Paul finished chewing and swallowed. "First, we have to find a reliable means of transportation."

"What about the boat?" asked Toshii.

"What boat?"

Toshii pointed over his shoulder. "The one docked at the pier."

The adults leaned to one side and glanced out the kitchen window. Sure enough, a thirty-foot Cobia 330 fiberglass pleasure boat sat two hundred feet away tied to a ten-foot pier. None of them had noticed it last night when they stumbled across the mansion and broke in.

"Yeah," replied Paul, again embarrassed that he had also overlooked the boat. "That'll do fine. Thanks, kid."

Toshii smiled.

"Assuming it works," Ed chimed in.

"We'll check it after breakfast." Paul spooned more of the eggs into his mouth.

"Where will we go?" asked Daphne.

Paul sipped some coffee. "Our best bet is to find a lightly populated coastal area and land there. Once on shore, we can make our way to a safe haven."

"Where would that be?" asked Akiko.

"I don't know. We'll have to figure that out later. Right now, the priority is getting out of here before the deaders catch us." Paul glanced over at Lisa. "You're welcome to join us."

Daphne's grip on his thigh tightened.

Lisa smiled. "Thank you for the offer, but I can't. My mother and daughter are waiting for me in Leesburg. I have to get back to them as soon as possible."

"Are they okay alone?" Ed asked.

Lisa shook her head. "My daughter is ten, and my mother is in her early seventies. She's in a wheelchair with the onset of dementia. My ex-husband agreed to watch them for a few days. Which reminds me. Does anyone have a cellphone I can borrow so I can check on them? I left mine in the limo."

Everyone had lost their phones escaping from the deaders. Ed pulled one out of his back pocket, but the screen had been shattered.

"Damn," Lisa mumbled.

Toshii reached into his pants pocket and withdrew a small leather case. Unzipping it, he removed a cellphone, turned on the power, and handed it to Lisa. "You can use mine."

"Thank you." Lisa took the phone, then leaned over and kissed Toshii on the head.

The boy stuck out his tongue. "Gross."

Lisa stood and headed into the living room.

"Do you think she'll get reception?" asked Daphne.

"Probably," replied Ed. "We're only on day three of the outbreak. It'll be a few more days before the power grid goes offline."

"In the meantime, we need to figure out where we're going from here." Paul slipped half a sausage link in his mouth and chewed.

"I don't recommend heading north," said Ed. "You have nothing but big cities and coastal communities until you hit northern Maine."

"Isn't it the same down south?" Daphne asked."

"Only down to Norfolk." Ed thought for a moment. "Then there's more open space once you get off the coast."

"Where's a good place to land?" asked Paul.

"Here." Toshii leaned over to the side and lifted a folder off the floor, which he handed to Paul.

Paul opened it. Inside were a few dozen 8x10 pieces of paper with Google Map satellite images. Most displayed patches of the United States from the Mississippi to the Atlantic, and from the tip of Florida to the Canadian border. Several showed the largest cities within two hundred miles of their location. The last four were close-ups of Annapolis, the peninsula they were on, and the roads leading north and east from the Chesapeake Bay.

"Where did you get these?" Paul asked as he thumbed through them.

"There was a computer in the room Mom and I were sleeping in. It wasn't passcode protected, and the Internet was still working, so I called up Google Maps and printed those out. I thought they might be useful."

"Good job, kid." Ed stepped up behind Toshii and rubbed his scalp.

Akiko hugged her child and kissed him on the cheek, eliciting a disgusted look from the boy.

"This is great." Paul placed the sheets back in the folder. "At least now we'll have an idea—"

Lisa screamed a single word from the living room. "Fuck!"

Everyone, including Gojira, jumped up from the table and ran into the other room, weapons at the ready to fight off deaders. Instead, they found Lisa with the cellphone still to her ear, kicking the back of the sofa so hard her foot tore through the fabric.

"What's wrong?" Paul asked.

"That fucking asshole ex abandoned my mother and daughter."

A Thank You to My Readers

I know I say this in every novel, but it's the truth. In addition to working for the CIA, writing has been one of the two most fulfilling things I've done with my life. The best part is having fans who read my books, enjoy them, and want more. I'm incredibly fortunate and grateful to have such a loyal fanbase. You keep reading and I'll keep writing.

If you enjoyed *The Ghosts of the Maria Doria*, please post a review on Amazon and/or Goodreads. Reviews drive the algorithms that get a writer's books more exposure on Amazon. It doesn't have to be long—just a rating and a sentence or two about why you liked or disliked it. To be successful in this genre, I need your support. Also, tell your friends about the book and post your review on Scott Baker's Realm of Zombies, Monsters, and the Paranormal (facebook.com/groups/1162724727634526).

If you enjoyed this book, pick up the first book in the series, *The Ghosts of Eden Hollow* and *The Ghosts of Salem Village*, the first two novels in the Tatyana paranormal saga. I'm plotting out and doing research for the fourth book. Hopefully, it'll be ready for release in the spring of 2023.

Thank you all in advance.

Acknowledgments

Non-writers think writing is hard. It's actually fun. The difficult part is the editing, making certain the details are accurate, and publishing the book. It's a complicated process involving many people, all of whom deserve to be recognized.

A huge debt of gratitude goes to Rhian Lockard. When I started researching *The Ghosts of Eden Hollow*, I had little understanding of the paranormal. Rhian spent an hour with me on the phone one evening explaining the reality of spiritual hauntings and spectral cleansings and answering all my questions. That background has been instrumental in writing these books. She's been extremely supportive. However, any errors in how to perform a cleansing, or any intentional diversions from reality for the sake of literary license (such as allowing spectral images to adopt corporeal form or mentally merging with a living person) are all on me.

The concept for this book came from a video I saw two years ago of a cruise liner caught at sea during a hurricane. Deep water is my phobia. Add to that being on a ship tossed around like a kid's toy in a bathtub. Include malevolent entities purposefully trying to sink you. I came up with (in my opinion) a terrifying plot. However, I did not know the first thing about ship operations or marine engineering. Thankfully, Jeff Thomson had spent time in the Coast Guard and agreed to read the book. The scenes about operating a cruise liner are much more accurate thanks to his advice.

The Tarot reading scene was virgin territory since I've never had one. Hadley Thorne and Jennifer Amato were extremely helpful in teaching me how a Tarot reading is performed and assisting me in setting up a card placement that fit perfectly with my plot scenario.

A major thanks go out to my beta readers who have been with me from book one, especially Dan Uebel and Doc Fried. They pointed out grammatical/spelling errors, plot flaws, and inconsistencies and offered their opinion on whether they liked the story. I would be lost without them.

Warren Design created the cover art for this book and both *The Ghosts of Eden Hollow* and *The Ghosts of Salem Village*. Their work perfectly fits the mood of this book. I'm looking forward to working with them in the future.

Finally, a significant debt of thanks goes to my family, human and furry. Working at home allows me to set my own hours. The pets are always there as my muses and my distractions. Roxie sits with me on my porch while I write during the day and, at night, when I'm in my study editing and managing social media, my cats Archer and Michonne stand in front of my desktop, Michonne because she wants to be petted and Archer to meow because he ran out of treats or because he can see the bottom of his food dish. Being a workaholic, I constantly put in more than forty hours a week. My family never complains (I think they're glad to get rid of me). I couldn't do this without their love, patience, and support.

About the Author

Scott M. Baker was born and raised in Everett, Massachusetts, and spent twenty-three years in northern Virginia working for the Central Intelligence Agency and traveling through Europe, Asia, and the Middle East. Scott is now retired and lives outside of Concord, New Hampshire, with his wife and fellow writer Alison Beightol, his stepdaughter, his mother-in-law, a stubborn but cuddly Boxer, and two cats who treat him as their human servant. In addition to his paranormal series, he is currently writing the *Nurse Alissa vs. the Zombies* and *The Chronicles of Paul* sagas, his latest zombie apocalypse series. Previous works include *Operation Majestic*, his Nazi time travel novel (think *Raiders of the Lost Ark* meets *Back to the Future* – with aliens); *Frozen World*, his stand-alone post-apocalyptic novel; the *Shattered World* series, his five-book young adult post-apocalypse thriller about a group of adventurers attempting to close interdimensional portals into Hell; *The Vampire Hunters* trilogy, about humans fighting the undead in Washington D.C.; *Rotter World*, *Rotter Nation*, and *Rotter Apocalypse*, his first post-apocalyptic zombie saga; *Yeitso*, his homage to the giant monster movies of the 1950s that he loved watching as a kid; as well as several zombie-themed novellas and anthologies.

Please check out Scott's social media accounts for the latest information on future books, upcoming events, and other fun stuff.

Facebook: Scott Baker's Realm of Zombies, Monsters, and the Paranormal:
facebook.com/groups/1162724727634526

Twitter:
twitter.com/vampire_hunters

YouTube:
youtube.com/channel/UC5AyCVrEAncr2E0N5XoyUdg/pla
ylists

Instagram:
instagram.com/scottmbakerwriter

TikTok:
tiktok.com/@authorscottmbaker

Blog:
scottmbakerauthor.blogspot.com

Wyrd Realities Homepage:
www.wyrdrealities.net/